SYMPTOMATIC

ALSO BY DANZY SENNA

Caucasia

A NOVEL

SYMPTOMATIC

Danzy Senna

RIVERHEAD BOOKS
a member of Penguin Group (USA) Inc.
NEW YORK
2004

This novel is a work of fiction. Names, characters, places, and incidents either are the product of the author's imagination or are used fictitiously, and any resemblance to actual persons, living or dead, businesses, companies, events, or locales is entirely coincidental.

For support during the writing of this book, the author wishes to thank the MacDowell Colony, the Mrs. Giles Whiting Foundation, and the College of the Holy Cross.

Riverhead Books
a member of
Penguin Group (USA) Inc.
375 Hudson Street
New York, NY 10014
www.penguin.com

Library of Congress Cataloging-in-Publication Data

Senna, Danzy.
Symptomatic / Danzy Senna.
p. cm.
ISBN 1-57322-275-5
1. Identity (Psychology)—Fiction. I. Title.
PS3569.E618S96 2004 2003066888
813'.54—dc22

Printed in the United States of America
1 3 5 7 9 10 8 6 4 2

This book is printed on acid-free paper. ♾

BOOK DESIGN BY JUDITH STAGNITTO ABBATE

SYMPTOMATIC

1

THIS WAS THE MOMENT I savored every night, when I could see him but he could not see me. I watched through the crack in the door as he moved around the kitchen, fixing us dinner. He was singing along to country music, this boy whose home I was temporarily calling my own. Strange, lovely boy. Sleepy blue eyes. Full pink lips. Tousled blond hair. Skin pale and milky. It irritated him, this skin. An unpleasant side effect of the medication. He'd grown used to the sensation, the permanent discomfort, he'd told me. It was just something he had learned to live with. But still. It looked uncomfortable.

I went inside. Shut the door softly behind me.

"Is that the one I love?"

"I don't know, is it?"

I pressed my body against his back and kissed the indentation at the back of his neck.

He turned around to look at me, examining my face with mock suspicion, as if I were a twin of myself. Then he smiled, touched my hair, tucked it behind my ear. "Hmmm, she looks like her. Does she taste like her?"

"Find out."

I closed my eyes and parted my lips and let his tongue

move inside. Red wine. It didn't take long before we were both entwined.

"I keep thinking you're going to disappear," he said, nuzzling his face against my neck, sniffing my skin like a dog. "Maybe I was dreaming when I met you and just haven't woken up. Because it doesn't seem real sometimes. You know? That you're here, living with me."

We met on the subway, me chewing my gum, trying to disappear behind a book. Him glancing at me every two minutes, blushing whenever our eyes met. A voice in my head had told me to stop glancing back. To stay away from that boy. *You know where that'll get you.* But I didn't listen.

Have you ever seen the end of a story before it even begins? Not like a psychic. But like somebody who keeps making the same mistake, because it feels good for a while, and even when it starts to feel bad it's a familiar kind of bad. A problem you can call your own.

Andrew was his name, but before I knew that I knew only what I saw: sympathy and seduction, old jeans and older money. Sensitive skin. When he found the courage to cross the car and asked me if I spoke Spanish, I'd smiled and said, *What makes you say that?* Answered a question with a question. The danger arises in that space. You know that as well as I do. The voice scolded me all the way home. *Now why'd you go and answer a question with a question? It's either yes or no. You either speak Spanish or you don't.*

I'd moved in with him one September night when the place I'd been living had become unbearable: a mold-infested women's boardinghouse in the mid-Thirties, where I'd fought chronic athlete's foot and mild bronchitis. It was 1992 and there weren't any institutions like it left in the city. All the others had been shut down years before, converted into health spas or luxury hotels. I imagined this one, too, wasn't long for the world. My room smelled vaguely of egg-salad sandwiches, and each night I lay awake listening to the sounds of communal living: coughs, vomiting from the resident bulimic, flushing toilets, sobbing from the girl next door, whom I wasn't sure I'd ever even laid eyes on. The place was all rules: a compulsory meal plan; a curfew; a "beau room" beneath the staircase, with a deck of cards and an incomplete Monopoly game, where you were supposed to entertain suitors. The official logo of the place hung in the lobby—a framed sketch of an older woman giving a younger woman a piggyback ride. The older woman, all bent over from the weight, wears a strained grin and is dressed like a schoolmarm—bun, clogs, floor-length dress buttoned to the collar; the younger woman is slender, swan-necked, and wears a flowered sundress and braids. She holds her arms loosely around the older woman's neck. Beneath them are the words "She ain't heavy . . . she's my sister." Everything about the place was designed to make you feel part of a community, but at night, in my twin bed, I felt a loneliness so complete it made my teeth hurt. A loneliness like grief, as if I were missing somebody who had died and would never come back.

One night Andrew walked me home from a movie. I was rushing to get back before curfew but paused on the stairs before I went inside.

"Please don't make me go back in there."

It was a joke, but he didn't take it as one.

"Okay," he'd said, not smiling. "I'll wait right here. Pack your bags."

He kept the cab waiting while I went upstairs and threw

my belongings into my Samsonite suitcase, stuffed my bedding into a garbage bag, and wrote the housemistress a note. I flew down the hall past bewildered housemates, shouting good-bye over my shoulder, then disappeared into the mild autumn air in a shining yellow cab.

The décor of his place was collegiate, preppy, hard angles and minimal furniture and stacks of books like leaning towers in every corner. A framed portrait of President Lincoln, something he'd picked up at a flea market, hung over his bed. On his bookshelf was a stack of vinyl records—Miles Davis stared down pensively, a witness to our coupling.

"Am I dreaming?" he asked. "I need to know."

"You're not dreaming. I'm really here."

"Prove it," he whispered.

LATER, I lay beside him, hands behind my head, telling him about my day at work.

"The usual shit," I said. "Just more contributions to the downfall of Western civilization."

It was my first job out of college. My title, at least, was special. The Carlton A. Riggs Fellowship for "young journalists of exceptional promise." Earlier that day I had stood on the subway platform at Rockefeller Center stopping businessmen wearing flowery ties. Was it a gift from a girlfriend or mother, or had they picked it out themselves? Did it mean they were comfortable with their masculinity? One tightly wound stockbroker thought I was calling him a faggot.

I told Andrew about the assignment. "Not quite Watergate."

"I'm sure that'll come."

He ran a finger down my stomach. "So tomorrow," he said, "my friend Sophie is having a birthday dinner at her place uptown. I want you to come. Will you do that?"

He had asked me to join him at similar events a few times before, but I always found excuses not to go. Every day in this new city I was trying to live in the purity of the present, free from context. Contexts, I knew, were dangerous: Once you put them in the picture, they took over.

Andrew believed it was unhealthy to keep things so separate. He had told me that if we continued to stay so isolated, removed from everything that had come before, the milk of our affection would start to curdle. It wasn't so much a warning as a plea.

He saw me hesitate now, and touched my chin. "Come on, I want you to meet my friends. I want them to meet you. It'll be good for us. You'll see. Like coloring in a picture." He paused. "Sometimes we feel like a sketch of something that's not filled in."

I looked at him. "Everything's so perfect right now. Maybe we should leave it this way." I smiled slightly. "A beautiful sketch."

He stroked my hair. "I know it seems perfect. And it is. To me too. But it can only get better." He sighed. "These friends, they're the closest thing I have to family. I mean, boarding school does that to you. And I guess I just want you to know them. And I want them to know you." He shrugged. "Is it wrong to want to show you off?"

"No." I touched his face. "I'm just being silly. Of course I'll go with you."

ə | 7

BEFORE I MOVED to this city, my mother and I had a conversation. She twisted herself into yoga contortions on a floor mat while I stood at the doorway, arms crossed, half turned away. She wanted to know why I would want to move here, the East Coast. Source of power. Why I would want to be a journalist at all. My mother doesn't believe in nonfiction. She doesn't believe there is such a thing as no agenda. Magazines, like the one I was heading off to work for, were, she said, bad for your health. They sustain the status quo in subtle, insidious ways. They keep us separated from each other, all the while homogenizing us into oblivion. I tried to explain to her what I loved about my work: The sense I got of disappearing into somebody else's story. Of watching and not being seen. Then and only then do the secrets reveal themselves to you. Silly girl, she said, as if that's possible—then shifted into a new asana.

2

SOPHIE OPENED THE DOOR wearing a silver Burger King tiara on her head. She kissed Andrew on the lips. "Welcome back to the land of the living!" She peeked behind him at me. "Well, let's have a look."

I stepped forward. Took her hand. Her eyes darted up and down me, taking in each detail of my clothes and hair. I couldn't read her verdict until she smiled. "Everybody's so curious to meet you. We knew Andrew was hiding something down there in the Village, but it was all so covert. We were beginning to suspect it was a man."

"No, not a man," I said, with a laugh.

"Well I can see that!" She took me by the arm and led me into the living room, casting a mischievous smile back at Andrew as she whispered to me, "Remind me to tell you about the time Andrew fell out of his dorm window, wearing a dress."

"What are you telling her?" Andrew wanted to know, his cheeks growing pink.

We both shook our heads, already in cahoots. "Nothing!"

There were five of them in the living room, lounging on the furniture, nursing their drinks. I stood before them, unsure what to do with my hands, while Sophie introduced me. Tommy, a pudgy fellow on the couch, held up his drink in my direction and sang, "Welcome to the Hotel Sophie. You can check out any time you like, but you can never leave."

"Don't scare her, Tommy. She hasn't even had a glass of wine."

Tommy ignored her and began to sing the Eagles now in drunken earnest.

"Her mind is Tiffany twisted, she's got the Mercedes bends, she's got a lot of pretty, pretty boys that she calls friends—"

A blond girl beside him, Chloe, hit him on the head with a pillow, then tackled him, holding her hand over his mouth so that the rest of the lyrics came out muffled, incoherent.

Andrew went around the room hugging the girls, doing elaborate handshakes with the boys. Everybody seemed happy to see him. They ruffled his hair. Slapped his butt. Made fun of his shoes. I watched him for a moment from where I stood near the door, actually glad now that I'd come. I liked seeing him in his natural habitat. He looked happy, but kept glancing back at me even as he worked the room.

Sophie grabbed my elbow and led me into the kitchen. I leaned against the counter, admiring the posh accoutrements, while she busied herself laying slices of smelly cheese on a platter. Over the stove hung a collection of expensive steel pots and pans on a metal rack. The refrigerator was made of brushed steel. The white counter behind me held a sleek, black espresso machine, an antique blender. The stove was German.

Andrew had explained to me that Sophie was an off-Broadway actress, and as I looked around I figured somebody else had to be paying the bills. My eyes settled on a purple flyer on the refrigerator advertising a play. The xeroxed picture showed Sophie wearing big nerdy glasses, Pippi Longstocking braids, her mouth open wide in a scream under the words "Critical Bitch: A One-Woman Show."

"So you're quite the mystery girl," she said, hands on hips, watching me. "Andrew has literally told us nothing about you. I mean, where'd you grow up?"

"California," I said. "Berkeley." I picked up a piece of cheese from the platter and popped it in my mouth.

She nodded at me sideways. "And where'd you go to college?"

I could see her mind working hard to place me—like a computer searching for a file that doesn't exist—the circle of pixel arrows that rotate but never point.

"California."

"University of—?"

I shook my head and told her the name of my alma mater. Private. Expensive. Her eyes brightened in relieved recognition. "Oh, wait. When did you graduate?" She knew people.

"Just this past spring."

She was a year older. She began to rattle off a bunch of names.

"Kyla Mallet."

"No."

"Peter Levy?"

"No."

"Alex Carmichael?"

"No."

She went on for a few more names but none of them struck a chord. And I missed my friends with a sudden, surprising intensity. Most of them had stayed in the Bay Area after graduation. My best friend, Lola, had gone to live in Mombasa, Kenya, on a Fulbright Scholarship. She was studying local art and culture. I'd since received sporadic postcards from her with details that made her seem very far away: She had picked up parasites and a six-inch worm had come out of her butt. She had taken to wearing a buibui and headscarf.

"Oh, well, must have been a different crowd," Sophie said, looking slightly perplexed. "And how did you and Mr. Andrew meet?"

I hesitated, trying to think of a more appropriate story. But my mind wasn't working, so I settled on the truth. "On the subway," I said. "He, well, he approached me."

"Wow," she said. "The only men who approach me on the subway are shaking a tin can from a wheelchair, or trying to sell me a yo-yo."

"I know. That's usually my story too. And normally I wouldn't have responded."

"But you knew a keeper when you saw one," she said, her head cocked slightly to the side. She sighed then, touched her forehead, tilted her head back, and said in a high, wistful voice, "Oh me, oh my. Where oh where is my Prince Charming?" Then she shrugged and added in a deeper voice, "Or at least a good fuck."

"Andrew," she said, as we entered the living room. "On the subway? You dog!"

AFTER DINNER we played charades. They'd all gone to Andover together once upon a time. Or "Bendover," as they preferred to call it. A few of their imitations were of people from school—a housemaster they all hated, the principal's secretary who was always drunk, a perverted philosophy teacher who liked to dress up as a pumpkin each Halloween. But for the most part, people chose to mimic an assortment of fallen celebrities: Dana Plato, Shirley MacLaine, John Belushi. When it came my turn I couldn't think of anybody obscure. And for no good reason I did Bruce Lee—leaping around the room doing a series of kicks and cuts close to but not touching people's faces.

After forty minutes or so, people were drunk and a little high, and the routines had become more and more ribald. People kept disappearing to get props from Sophie's bedroom. Jeanie, a curly-haired publicist, came out wearing a leotard, and she gyrated around the room until somebody guessed Jennifer Beals from *Flashdance*.

When it was Sophie's turn, she affected an indignant expression and began walking around with her butt stuck out and her hands on her hips, eyeing each of the guests and chewing imaginary gum as if it were cud, shaking her head. Everybody stared at her, dumbfounded.

"Sophie, you gotta do better than that."

She started laughing and said, "You're right." She grabbed a couple of pillows from the couch, and disappeared into the hallway.

While we waited, they played a game where they reenacted a whole scene from the movie *The Breakfast Club*. Word for word. Gesture for gesture. Andrew whispered to me that it was called "Custodial Arts." They had played it in high school. Now they fell easily back into the old routine, each one taking up their assigned role in the production. Chloe was Molly Ringwald. Andrew played the Emilio Estevez role. I sat quietly laughing at them all—their sole audience.

And it seemed they could have gone on reciting the

whole movie, but after about ten minutes Tommy let out a shout. “Good God!” he said, pointing toward the door. We all turned to look.

Sophie stood, arms held in the air, transformed. She had rubbed something—maybe shoe shine—all over her face. She’d put bright orange lipstick around the edges of her mouth. And when she turned around in a fashion-plate pirouette, I saw she’d punctuated her behind with twin pillows she’d strapped on with a belt. She strutted into the center of the room and began shaking her head and sucking her teeth and talking in a voice that wasn’t her own. We weren’t allowed to talk in charades as a rule, but nobody stopped her.

“How many times I gots to tell you?” she drawled. “Sheeyit. Don’t be leavin them tampons soakin’ in the toilet for my ass to clean up. I ain’t yo’ mama. And another thing. Yo skinny ass be leavin’ paypah towels all over the fuckin’ sink and you think I got time to clean up that shit?” She turned and scratched her pillow-clad bottom.

When I looked at Andrew, he was laughing until tears were streaming down his cheeks. So was the rest of the room. They all knew who it was she was imitating, but they were not saying it, allowing her to continue the routine a little longer. When she began to mime mopping a floor, singing in a deep voice “Swing Low, Sweet Chariot,” they all shouted in unison, “ ’Retha!” Then collapsed into laughter and scattered applause.

Sophie whipped around. “Finally!” She slumped down into an armchair. “For God’s sake. Could it have been any more obvious?”

Andrew said, “We just wanted to watch the show a little longer.” Then he turned to explain to me, “ ’Retha was this insane cleaning lady who used to do the dorms at school. She was, like, four hundred pounds and always mumbling about how much she hated us as she cleaned up the bathroom."

Tommy, beside me, added, "My God. Do you remember her husband? He used to pick her up on Fridays? He looked like he'd just stepped out of the federal penitentiary. He had a Jheri Curl and drove a Chrysler LeBaron."

"Oh right, what was his name again?" Chloe, wiping the tears off her cheeks, wanted to know.

"LaVonne or Laroo something," said Len, a wiry kid with a tousled mop of black curls. "The names. The names. Remember when I subbed in the public schools that one semester? God. I remember I had three Keishas in my classroom and they all spelled their names wrong—the most bizarre variations."

"I think it's kind of cool," said Estelle, a wan blond girl by the fire. "Creative."

"The real question is," Sophie said, standing up and undoing the straps that held the pillows to her behind, "are those names supposed to be creative, or is it all just kind of an epic spelling mistake? Like dyslexia on a mass scale?"

The room was silent for a beat, seeming to ponder the question. Then Tommy leaned forward in his seat with sudden excitement and said, "All right. So get this. I was watching a rerun of *The Newlywed Game* a few weeks ago."

Somebody groaned, like maybe he'd told this story before. He ignored them.

"Anyway, this big fat black lady was on it. I mean huge. And Bob Eubanks asks all the women to answer this question: 'Where's the craziest place you and your husband have ever made whoopee?' "

Sophie began to titter. "Oh my God. Whoopee."

"So all the other women go down the line blushing, giggling, saying things like 'the kitchen table,' 'his office,' 'the gym.' You know, typical places. Then he gets to the big black lady. And she thinks for a moment—real hard—then says, 'Uh, I'ze gon' hafta say in da butt.' "

The entire group exploded into laughter around me. Sophie leaned forward and slapped Tommy on the thigh. "You are so bad."

"What? Come on!" Tommy said. "It was funny."

Andrew's face was flushed with affectionate pleasure as he smiled at his friends. He glanced at me and squinted, his eyes flickering something—a vague remembrance, like he knew me from somewhere and was trying to remember my name.

"Hey," he said, and reached for my hand, but I was already standing, heading out of the room. I found the bathroom at the end of the hall and shut myself inside. Fancy skin products were lined aggressively on the sink counter. Exfoliating scrubs. Clay masques. Moisturizing creams. Milk cleansers. I recalled a joke I'd heard as a child. Your epidermis is showing! The big kids used to say it to the little kids, just to watch them burn with shame as they searched themselves for the private part they'd left exposed.

I turned on the water full blast for no reason, and opened the medicine cabinet. I pulled out some of Sophie's La Prairie eye cream with collagen and sniffed the contents. Its scent was expensive, weak, barely there. There were lots of pills. Prescriptions. A douche. Tweezers. A diaphragm container. I closed the cabinet and saw the mirror had steamed up from the hot water. I drew the outline of a face in the fog. I had been doodling this same face since I was a little girl, on napkins and glass, an anxious tic I resorted to whenever I felt out of place. It was a crude sketch of a woman. She had big eyes with long lashes, a long nose, full bow lips, and wavy lines around her face to signify hair. Ambiguous. Guarded. There was a certain refracted quality to the features that made her hard to place. I don't know who she was supposed to be—only that her face calmed me, like an old friend who shows up at just the right moment. Now I watched the fingerprints that were her fade into the mirror.

After that I sat for a while on the tiled floor near the window, hugging my knees. The glass on it was pebbled, blind. I opened it and breathed in the cold wet air. The rain was coming down pretty hard. We were on the sixth floor, and down below I could see the tops of umbrellas moving past—a procession of West Side couples. I shut my eyes and listened. The rain in the leaves sounded like a fireplace crackling.

I thought of things I could do or say—things I'd already said and done. But I was all of a sudden so sleepy. I yawned, literally unable to move from my seat by the window. I curled up on that cold tiled floor and closed my eyes. And I started to fall asleep. Me, the insomniac. A profound heaviness came over me. In the dream I was babysitting for somebody else's child. A baby, no more than a few months old. I'd put it down on a bed to sleep, but had somehow lost it under the sheets and comforter. I heard the baby's smothered cries, but no matter how many blankets I ripped away, I could not find the baby. I was frightened, not of the baby suffocating but of the mother coming home to find what I'd done.

I woke to a sharp knocking.

"Everything okay in there?" Andrew called through the door.

"Yeah." My voice was groggy.

"We're getting ready to serve the cake. You coming?"

"In a sec."

"You sure everything's okay, babe?"

A sound like laughter from my throat. "I'm sure."

Have you ever seen the end of the story before it begins?

"Well, all right." He sounded worried. He had seen the look on my face—the look of somebody on the verge of extinction.

"I miss you," he whispered into the crack. A second later I heard his footsteps moving away down the hall.

When I got up and looked in the mirror, there were lines on my cheeks, a faint grid of squares where the tiled floor had pressed into my face. It made me look old, wrinkled on one side. I ran my fingers across the impression, wondering if it would fade by the time I reached the party.

MY FATHER did not approve of my decision to move here, either. He told me so one day last spring while we stood in line at a grocery store. He pointed at the magazine, my future, where it sat on the rack, and told me in no uncertain terms what was wrong with the cover image—why it was problematic. That was the word he used. Problematic. I saw what he saw and agreed with his analysis—but, I told him, that only proves that they need more people like me on the inside. People who can identify a problem, name it, fix it. He smiled and shook his head and started unloading groceries. But it seeps inside, baby doll, he said. It seeps inside.

3

HAT NIGHT, I lay curled in the corner of Andrew's mattress, my back to him. Outside, I could hear a strong wind bashing across garbage bins, and far distant voices disappearing into it.

Andrew leaned over me and touched my hair. He tried to kiss my neck. His breath smelled of Chartreuse and birthday cake. "You make me so happy. Do you know that?"

I examined my fingernails. There were little white flecks in the pink. Some kind of vitamin deficiency. I'd have to look it up.

He went on. "Sophie thought you were great. She told me so." He tucked a strand behind my ear. "Thanks for coming. I know it was a little awkward for you, not knowing anybody, but it meant a lot to me." He pressed in tighter against me, and I could feel his desperation. He could feel me slipping away. He whispered, "My life is so much better with you around. I was—so—sad—before you came along."

I looked at his wrist where it lay flung before my face. His veins were thick and visible, the blue resting so close to the surface. And above them I could make out the faint scar.

He had been infatuated with a girl—the daughter of a diplomat, named Flavia. When she broke up with him, he carved her name into his wrist with a jackknife. He lost blood but survived the cut, and spent the next year in a hospital outside of Boston, called McLean. That's where he'd first been prescribed the medication that made him itch and tremble. If you looked closely enough you could make out an *F* and an *L*. He had told me the story the first night we slept together, in the monotonous tone of somebody who has had too much therapy. He had rehearsed this disclosure in counselor's quarters. I'd wanted every detail, but he was reticent and only wanted me to know that he had since learned to "moderate his emotions."

I touched the scar. "Do you think you'll be on that medicine your whole life?"

He loosened his hold slightly and was quiet, just breathing for a moment. He often seemed embarrassed by the fact of his dependency on the medication, no matter how well he'd learned to divulge it.

"Who knows," he finally said. "Maybe. Oh, I don't know." He stroked my hair. "I've always been sad. Ever since I can remember. It's like I've been in mourning since the day I was born. But you—you make everything better. New." He paused. "It's mysterious, isn't it?"

"It is," I said, turning to look at his face.

His eyes were a strange color. An opaque swirl of gray and blue. They looked odd to me, half-blind, like the eyes of a newborn, before they turn a more ordinary, permanent shade of brown. And I thought about how sometimes another body beside you in bed—the heat and weight of it—can make you feel more alone, not less.

He slid his hand under my shirt and rested it on my belly. "I love you," he said.

I opened my mouth to say something but he touched my lips.

"Shhh. I just want you to know."

I WOKE THE NEXT MORNING before dawn. Andrew slept heavily beside me. His writing day wouldn't begin for many hours. I stared at his face while he slept. His hair was stuck to his forehead with sweat. His cheeks were flushed, his brows raised as if he'd been surprised by something in his sleep.

I slid out of bed, showered, and got dressed in the dark of the living room. Outside, the light was faint, barely there, just a hue in the sky. I always found half-lights more blinding than utter darkness, and my eyes didn't know which way to adjust.

Winter was coming. I could feel it. Drizzle lay like a veil across my face. All along the way, out of the corner of my eye I saw things that made me twitch and gasp. A wet, pink fetus curled in the gutter, that was really just a raw chicken wing. A severed finger lying between two trash cans, that upon closer inspection was really a steak fry with ketchup on the tip. A puddle of colorful vomit that was just that.

I stared into the faces of the women I saw, studied them as if they were road signs—warnings of what lay up around the bend.

"Do Not Enter," read one woman's face.

"Slow Down," said another.

Once the game started, I couldn't stop.

Blind Corner, Merge Left, No Passing, Stay Clear, No Thru Traffic, Soft Shoulder, Dead End. I saw disappointment in the deep lines etched around a mouth. Rage in the cracks between the eyebrows. Wide eyes signified a bewildered hurt. A jaw jutting forward spoke of unfulfilled desire.

I wore only the corduroy jacket I'd brought with me from California. By the time I got to Midtown, I was shivering. The doors to the office building were still locked. I had to knock on the glass to get the attention of the security guard.

Upstairs, I headed down the hall toward my office, with my face turned down. As I rounded the corner I nearly crashed into a cleaning lady pushing a cart of equipment. We both jumped in fright. I had never seen her before. I had never come to work this early. She was tiny, with skin the color of molasses, and she wore a net over her straightened silver hair. She was old enough to be my grandmother.

"I'm sorry," I said, touching my chest.

She chuckled. "Don't be, baby. Don't be." Then disappeared down the hall.

Back at my desk, I scanned the classifieds for leads on a new place to live.

4

NDREW WATCHED ME with anxious eyes all week. He wanted to know what was the matter. I told him I was coming down with something. It was true. But it was a nameless illness, yet unformed, and I didn't bother going to a doctor. In bed, I shrank away from his touch. No stirring of desire when he kissed me. His tongue in my mouth felt like a dentist's instrument. I told him I had my period when I didn't, and lay stiffly on the farthest edge of his mattress, not touching. He didn't argue, but I could see he suspected the problem was more than blood.

At night, I lay awake for hours listening to my body speak to me: the grumbles and aches and pricks and itches—evidence, I suspected, of a problem growing larger inside of me.

By day I continued to call numbers I found in the classifieds and to go look at shares after work. But I found a reason to turn down each potential home. The reasons weren't hard to find. One woman had a grizzled boyfriend who sat on the couch in boxer shorts cutting his toenails while she showed me around. Another had an alphabetized system of arranging cans on her shelves. A third, an environmentalist, told me that one of her house rules was that I couldn't flush the toilet unless I had made a bowel movement.

"If it's yellow, let it mellow," she said, smiling down into the golden toilet water. "If it's brown, flush it down."

I COMPLAINED to Carlos the mailman, who stopped by my desk on his delivery route. Carlos was caramel-colored, with black wavy hair and a "Dominican Forever" tattoo on his forearm. He smelled of Drakkar Noir.

"Am I missing something here?" I waved the classified page at him. "Other people have homes in this city. At least most of them. Where did they find them?"

He slapped a pile of junk mail on my desk. "Welcome to the Big Shitty."

Carlos hated New York. Apparently, when he was a teenager in the Bronx, he had designed a T-shirt that said, in simple white letters, "Why are we here?" over a small picture of a rotten apple with a worm poking out of one side. He'd printed a hundred of them up, and sold exactly one—to his mother. He claimed he still had four boxes of them in his basement.

Carlos wanted to move to California. He had never been there, but swore someday he would go. He was going to see "that golden bridge" before he died.

He liked talking to me, mainly because I was from the other coast. He would loiter beside my desk, staring down at me with starstruck eyes, asking me questions about Los Angeles, paying no mind to the fact that I was from the Bay Area. How much was the rent for a one-bedroom in Malibu? What were the cool nightclubs in L.A.? Could you really find a parking spot anywhere? And his favorite subject: What famous people had I seen? He made me tell him over and over again about the time I stood in line behind Donald Sutherland at a Pep Boys.

"I must be missing something," I said now, resting my face in my hands, glaring down at the listings for shares. "Some secret apartment source."

"Don't you know, *chica*?" he said with a snort. "Everything good in this stupid-assed city comes from a secret source. It's called connections. Nothin' random about that. You gotta know the right people."

"What if you don't?"

"You make some friends, sister," he said, trudging out the door with his cart. "You make some friends mighty quick."

BURIED UNDER all the junk Carlos left was a postcard from Mombasa showing a grinning woman in traditional garb on a dirt road.

> *Dear Bootsy Collins, I have lost twenty-five pounds—best diet in the world, those worms. I dreamt about you last night. Only you were Marlo Thomas on* That Girl, *bangs and all. You were swirling around Midtown in a trench coat, laughing your head off. Is it true? Love, Lola.*

THERE WAS A MESSAGE blinking out at me from my computer's inbox a few days later. A fact-checker in the business department—Greta Hicks—had overheard me complaining to Carlos about my apartment search. She knew of a sublet that had just become available in Brooklyn. She told me the price and it was well within my range. Was I interested?

We met at eight-thirty the next morning at the Au Bon Pain a block away from our office. The café was a chaos of commuters, and I stood at the door for a moment, searching for Greta among their faces. There she was, seated in the back. Forty-something. Teetering between voluptuous and overweight. Olive skin, straight dark hair streaked with a few strands of white. A faint shadow of a mustache over her lip. She was looking at herself in a compact mirror, grinning as she checked her teeth for bits of food.

I'd met Greta before, at a brown-bag luncheon for new employees we'd both attended over the summer. There had been an unusually large influx of hires starting in July—writers, reporters, fact-checkers, and me—and they lumped us all together for the session. We spent three hours in an airless conference room, picking at stale potato chips and taking tepid bites of our turkey wraps while a stream of superiors came in to talk to us about everything from health insurance policies to journalistic ethics. I recalled feeling sorry for Greta, because she was so much older than all the rest of us. She was also overdressed in a mauve pantsuit, wore a sad red carnation on her lapel, and had the enthusiasm of an adult-education student, raising her hand at every lull to ask a question.

At the end of the meeting we stood around in clusters, mingling, and Greta walked around handing everybody a Hershey's Kiss. I remember appreciating the gesture, ridiculous as it was. I'd been feeling particularly uncomfortable that day—a slight chill from the other hires when they looked at my name tag with "Riggs Fellow" emblazoned boldly under my name—a chill that never quite went away. I'd felt a familiar insecurity—that I did not belong here. That, in fact, I was an impostor, that all my credentials were indeed a fiction, and any day now I would be discovered and expelled from this world. Greta, too, had seemed out of place, and so we ended up standing together while the other staffers huddled and bonded. Since then, we had passed one another in the hall, once we'd chatted by the water cooler about the weather, but as she worked in a different department, we never followed up on that initial encounter.

Now she glimpsed me and raised her arm to wave as I approached, and I saw dark half-moons under her arms, new or old sweat, I couldn't be sure.

"Ah," she said when I was in front of her. "Here she is." She pushed a steaming paper cup in my direction. "Green tea okay?"

"Thanks," I said, a bit surprised. "How'd you know?"

"Just a lucky guess. I remembered you saying you were from California." She took a sip from her coffee cup, then sat back and smiled at me, her eyes twinkling, humorous, as if she'd just told a joke.

"Well, finally!"

Finally what? I was confused. "Am I late?"

"No, no," she shook her head. "It's just, well, I never see you anymore. Ever since that meeting last summer, you've been this beige blur darting past me in the in the lobby, chasing this story or that."

"Maybe that's how I look—but I'm not chasing anything good, I can assure you."

"Really? Well, I'm sure they're just priming you for bigger and better things. I mean, the fellowship is a big deal. I saw that little item they ran about you this summer."

"Oh, that," I said, slightly embarrassed. The staff newsletter had run a short profile during my first week, along with a goofy snapshot of me sitting behind my desk, looking slightly alarmed. It had made the Riggs Fellowship sound like a big deal, all right. I'd seen the bitterness in the other reporters' smiles. Now I waved my hand. "All lies. Yellow journalism."

"Well, I'm impressed, that's all."

Easily impressed. I took a sip of tea. It scalded my tongue. "Anyway," I said, "about the apartment."

"Right," she said, and paused for a moment, looking at me sideways. "So what's the big rush? You sounded urgent when you were talking to Carlos."

Clearly whatever she'd overheard had made me sound desperate. I didn't blame her for asking. She'd only met me once, really, and there were a lot of odd ducks out there in the rental market.

I explained now, in as vague terms as I could get away with: "I moved in with a guy a few months ago, but it was too early. We didn't know each other that well at the time."

She nodded, female empathy softening her features. "Ah, and now you do."

"Yeah, now I do."

"I had a feeling it was something like that. I saw you in the cafeteria the other day looking, well, pretty downcast."

I hadn't known it was that obvious, noticeable even to virtual strangers. But now that she said it, I felt a lurch of sadness—so strong I had to look away. I recalled the last meal he'd cooked for me. We'd eaten it side by side in bed, a trashy thriller flickering on the television set before us. And the indigo scarf he'd bought for me one afternoon, on a whim, during his neighborhood wanderings, just to see the color against my skin.

"I'll survive," I said, trying to smile, but my face felt like hardened wax, impossible to move.

"Of course you will!" she said, then pulled out a small slip of paper. "Now, the apartment."

She went into the details, something about her hairdresser's cousin who had left town abruptly for six months. The hairdresser was supposed to water her plants and take in the mail, but he lived all the way uptown, and the apartment was in Brooklyn, and so he was hoping to rent it out cheap to somebody reliable who would be responsible and didn't mind leaving when the girl came back. The best part was that the girl had been living in the apartment for many years under rent control, and so the rent was way below market price.

"It's not that far a trip to work, and from what he said, it's a good space. It's in a"—Greta smirked as she made quote marks—" 'transitional neighborhood,' so you can still get your cappuccino in the mornings. Or green tea." Her eyes flickered to my paper cup, and she smiled. "Yes, I suppose you could even get green tea." She paused. "But maybe you want something that's, you know, a little more upscale."

I shook my head. She had the wrong idea about me. They all did. "It sounds perfect," I said. "I'm not picky about the space, just about who I have to share it with." I told her about a few of my recent flurry of potential roommates, and she laughed. "Oh no, we mustn't let you end up with one of those."

Afterward, we walked back to the office together through the drizzle, sharing her umbrella. It was battered, loose on a few spokes, and said "Chase Manhattan" across the blue vinyl—something she'd no doubt gotten as a gift from the bank years ago. She chattered about the rental market, meaningless banter, and I tried to hold up my end of the conversation, but there was a soreness in my throat and an ache in my bones.

We took the elevator up together. The plan was that I would call her hairdresser that evening, after she'd had a chance to talk to him. At her floor, she stood between the open doors for a moment, looking back at me. She scratched her head. "Listen, I hate to ask, but you aren't going to have a change of heart and move back in with this guy next week, are you?" She emitted an anxious little laugh. "I mean, are you sure it's over? For good?" She looked pained after she said it, and a flush of color came to her cheeks.

I paused, and asked myself the same question. "Yes, I swear. It's over for good." It was a promise to myself as much as to her.

"I thought so. I'm sorry I asked."

"No, please. It only makes sense."

She smiled, then touched my arm. "I'll let Jiminy know he can trust you."

"Thank you."

"Don't mention it." She began to go, but turned back. "You know, it's true what they say. Time is the only thing that heals these breakups. And you're so young, hon. You've got nothing but time."

"I know," I said, a little more coldly than I'd intended. She was only trying to be kind, but the aphorism felt more like a reminder of the endless solitary nights I saw stretched out before me.

My family would not have approved of Andrew. The last time I brought a boy like him home, they were pleasant to his face, but later, alone with me, expressed their bewilderment.

"What do you have to talk about?" my mother wondered as she kneaded dough at the kitchen table.

My father, pulling weeds out of the backyard: "I didn't know they made those anymore."

My brother, waxing his surfboard on the other side of the lawn: "They don't."

5

THE APARTMENT WAS dark and empty when I got home from work.

I didn't turn on the lights. Instead, I went to the phone to call the number Greta had given me.

A man answered on the fourth ring, just when I was about to hang up.

"Yo," he said.

"Is this Jiminy?"

"Yeah."

I told him who I was: Greta Hicks's friend calling about the apartment.

He paused. Inhaled something. Held it in as he said in a tight voice, "Oh. Uh-huh. She called me about you. Right. So you want it or what?"

Did I want it? I had never seen the place. "I'm interested," I said. "Can you describe it?"

"Describe it? Shit, I don't know. It's an apartment. You know, nothing fancy, but it'll do."

"How big?"

"Um, I guess it's about, you know, two bedrooms. Nah. One bedroom." He sighed. "Yo, G, I can't describe this shit. Bitch didn't tell me I'd have to describe it. It's chill. *Real* chill. And yo, you ain't gonna find a better deal that close to Manhattan. Know what I'm sayin', son? This ain't no joke."

I'd met people like Jiminy before. The childish nickname, the exaggerated slang, the wild defensiveness were all too familiar. I also knew I had to tiptoe, because the fact was, he had something I thought I wanted. I would simply have to put up with his foolishness. For the remainder of the conversation, he continued to address me as "son" and "G." After some hemming and hawing he agreed to let me see the space before I committed. I didn't look forward to meeting him in person, but I reminded myself that if things worked out, I would only have to meet him once.

We made plans for the following night, after he had finished doing hair for the day.

I hung up and stood for a moment in the kitchen, biting a hangnail that had begun to irritate me.

"You're leaving me."

I turned. Directly ahead, through the double doors, Andrew sat in the darkened living room on the couch, watching me. It seemed strange that I had not seen him before.

"I knew something was up."

I approached him slowly, sat down beside him, reached out for his hand. He pulled it away.

"What? I don't make you happy?" His eyes were shining.

I raked a hand through my hair. "I—this was supposed to be temporary. Remember? Just till I found a place of my own."

"But why didn't you tell me you were planning to move out?"

I slid my hands under my thighs, rocked forward slightly. "I didn't plan it. Somebody at work knew of a sublet. It just sort of fell into my lap today—the opportunity, so I thought I'd check it out. You know this city. You can't sleep on these deals."

The words floated in the space before me, a cloud of bullshit.

"You're a liar," he said. "You've been looking this whole time, haven't you?"

I didn't answer the question. Instead, I stared out the window. In the building adjacent to Andrew's, I could see into an apartment. A woman was sitting at her kitchen table, eating something white and gooey out of a giant mixing bowl. She had dark hair and horn-rimmed glasses and ate with what looked like a giant wooden spoon. I couldn't see the other end of the table. She kept looking up and smiling, as if somebody was there, but for some reason I got the feeling she was alone.

"I need to be in my own space," I said. "Don't take it personally. Please."

He looked at me. In the dark, his face looked pale as a dish, cracked down the middle. "It was the party, wasn't it? That's when things started changing. After that night. You didn't like my friends."

I looked away, at the rug, the swirl of orientalism and dirt. I wondered what Lola was doing in Kenya right now. I imagined her squatting over a dirt hole, hoisting her buibui up around her middle while she relieved herself of worms. If she could see me now.

I glanced up. Andrew was still waiting for an explanation.

"You're right," I said. "I didn't like your friends. I didn't know enough about you. And you didn't know enough about me either. We jumped into this too fast. We should have taken it in stages, gotten to know each other first. We should have done it in the right order."

"The right order," he said. "What does that mean? Boy meets girl on a subway. It's love at first sight, the way it only happens in the movies, the way it never happens in a city as big and brutal as this. And then one day the girl walks out without an explanation. Destroys everything for no good reason. Is that what you mean by the right order?"

"Maybe," I said, hugging my stomach. "Maybe that's what I mean."

He rubbed his face, quite violently, as if he were trying to get something off it. Afterward he stared at me in hard silence for a while. When he finally spoke, it was to say, "You want to hear something weird? Maybe you can help me figure it out. In all the months I've known you, I've never been able to remember what you look like. Isn't that bizarre? I used to think it was a good thing, the suspense I felt going to meet you in public—this completely irrational fear I had that I might not recognize you. But it's something else, isn't it?"

I looked back out the window. The woman in the apartment was laughing now, tittering into her hand as if somebody had just told a wickedly funny joke.

"Are you listening to me?"

I looked back. Nodded. "Yes, you were saying my face is hard to remember."

He made a mocking sound in his throat, as if I'd given him the wrong answer on a quiz. Then said, "Tell me something. Is this the way it always goes with you?"

I shrugged. "I've been here before."

He watched me for a moment, then whispered, "Who are you?"

I didn't say anything. I just stared at him in the dark for a moment, thinking of all the different answers to this question I had already given. You know how it goes. The disclosure, followed by the edifying speech. My body, the lesson.

But I just rubbed my eyes, yawned. "It's late. I'm tired."

I slept on the couch that night—shivering under a scratchy plaid blanket. From behind Andrew's bedroom door, I could hear the drone of a grunge band he liked. The music played over and over again on auto repeat until morning.

My father's subject: the relationship between history and the individual. He believes everybody is an "excretion" of his or her environment. That's the word he uses. *Excretion.*

6

T WAS NOT YET DARK in Brooklyn, drizzling slightly, a netting of moisture that lent the neighborhood an impressionist softness as I made my way up DeKalb Avenue. I followed the directions I'd scribbled on a napkin.

The neighborhood was "transitional," as Greta had described. Behind every ghetto façade lurked subtle hints of gentrification. A soul food restaurant had posted a sign advertising its new vegetarian menu. The bodega I passed sold *The New York Times*. A gated community garden had sprung up in the shadow of a giant housing project. Sprinkled amid the bald-headed b-boys were dreadlocked intellectuals wearing tiny, wire-rimmed glasses and kente-cloth scarves. And a few nervous white people, too, walking swiftly toward the light of the subway, hunched over as if hiding something in their coats, eyes twitching back and forth, on guard against phantom muggers.

I was meeting the hairdresser, Jiminy, at six. I was a few minutes early and stood in front of the red brick building shifting my feet and staring across the street at a drug transaction in progress. A cluster of art student types were chatting nervously with a slender, dark-skinned boy who held a brindled pit bull puppy on a thick chain leash. I watched the secret handshake, glimpsed the baggie passed between them, before the students all climbed into their battered Toyota Corolla and drove away, their eyes wide with nervous excitement. The dealer stuck the money in his pocket, got into a gargantuan silver Jeep with tinted windows—the dog in the back—and put on some music. I listened to the bass thudding against the glass and felt a pang of longing for Andrew's warm alcove of an apartment. I tried to imagine coming home to the stern brick building behind me every night after work.

Just then I heard somebody say, "Yo, son, you ready to see this shit or what?"

I turned to see a young man—platinum blond hair, pale, pugnacious face—standing before me. He wore a huge parka with a fur collar, jeans three sizes too large bagged around his legs like empty sacks. His skin was ruddy, pink, his features coarse and belligerent. He cupped his hand around a cigarette and looked nervously over his shoulder at the rocking, thudding Jeep. "We gotta do this quick. 'Cause I'm in a hurry. I got to meet this motherfucker at seven and his ass is gonna go ape shit if I'm late. Know what I'm sayin', son?"

INSIDE, I followed Jiminy up a drab staircase, while he explained the situation to me. His cousin, Vera, whose apartment it was, had left the country recently. She had moved to London to try to make it as a singer.

"She been trying for years here, but motherfuckers don't be payin' her on time, and her band members be pullin' all sorts of trifling shit, so she just got the fuck out. She knew somebody in London and so homegirl just up and split. Without telling none of them mofos."

"Sounds like a smart move," I said, just to say something. "Hope it works out."

"Shit, I hope it works out too," he said. "Hope she stays there and gets rich and fucking famous and remembers her lil' cuzzy-cuz, Jiminy. Know what I'm sayin'?"

When we got to the sixth floor, he fiddled with his janitor-sized ring of keys in front of a door marked 6C. "She owes me," he said. "That's for damn sure. That bitch always be leaving me to clean up her shit. Ever since we was little. Just last week, she called me from the fuckin' airport askin' me to find her a subletter. I said, yo, son, you gots to be kidding. But the bitch wasn't kidding. So here I am."

He finally found the right key and unlocked the door. We stepped into the darkness. I noticed a smell—like curdled perfume. It overwhelmed me for the briefest moment—then faded into something more bearable.

He turned on the lights, then went and stood by the living room window with his forehead pressed against the glass, jingling his keys noisily around in his pocket and listening to his Walkman. The sounds of a manic rapper leaked out from his headphones. I waited for him to lead me on the tour, but he just stared, forlorn, out at the street life he no doubt yearned to be a part of. I moved on to explore the space alone.

Hardwood floors. A mantelpiece over a fireplace. A kitchenette looking into the living room. An ordinary one-bedroom walk-up. The décor was unobtrusive. And in fact, as I looked around, the entire apartment had a half-finished quality. I imagined the girl moving in with hopes of a robust social life—raucous dinner parties around the kitchen table with friends, romantic Sunday mornings spent curled on the couch with a lover. But these hopes had been abandoned and what was left was a blunt space meant to serve single lonely desires. A plywood bookshelf sat half-assembled in a corner, a screwdriver resting on its lowest shelf. One wall in the kitchen had been painted a cheery terra-cotta orange, but the rest of the walls had been left white. A set of expensive pots and pans sat on the stove, but they looked as if they had never been used—the largest pot serving as a container for a handful of takeout menus. The silverware drawer was filled with ketchup and mustard packets, disposable chopsticks, fortune cookies, plastic forks and knives.

A two-cup coffeemaker sat on the kitchen counter, with a ring of darkness around its glass bottom. In the refrigerator, I found a half-empty bottle of cheap Chilean chardonnay, a moldy lump of brie in Saran Wrap, a can of condensed sweetened milk.

I thought about Andrew's refrigerator. Since the day I'd moved in, it had been stocked to the gills with fresh fruits and vegetables, fine wines, cheeses. Frozen hunks of meat in the freezer. The sizzle of oil in the pan and the sound of Thelonious Monk greeted me each evening when I approached his door.

Living here, would I resort to a diet like the one in the refrigerator before me—a permanent cocktail party nibbled alone in front of the television set each night?

In the bathroom, I found more vestiges of the other girl's life. Tampons rested beside the toilet. A clutter of drugstore makeup—crumbling Maybelline eye shadow, Revlon Toast of New York lipstick—sat abandoned on the counter. There was a tangle of dark hair in the bathtub sieve where she had not bothered to clean before she left town. In each corner of the tub was a votive candle, and for some reason this fact made me sad, thinking of the girl pampering herself in the dark.

The bedroom was the least lived-in. A stark, white duvet was thrown over the bed. All the sheets were white, too. A single dying white orchid sat beside the bed, in a white ceramic holder with holes in it that revealed the soil. It rested on top of a book, *The Dance of Anger: A Woman's Guide to Changing the Patterns of Intimate Relationships.* I picked it up. It was a library book. I opened it. Three months overdue.

There was a tackboard with postcards, receipts, a Map to the Stars' Homes, the kind you can buy all over Los Angeles, and an expired gift certificate for Estée Lauder stuck to it, but no pictures graced the walls.

In the closet I found a pair of scuffed black leather boots with rings of last winter's salt around the toes and ankles. Clothes she'd left behind: a corduroy blazer, a red acrylic/wool scarf, and a leather motorcycle jacket with metal studs on the shoulders. And something funny: two silver wraparound dresses, exactly alike, only in different sizes. They were cheap quality, and the smaller one had the price tag still hanging off of it, showing she'd bought it on sale. She must have bought it for a smaller friend. Or maybe for herself—incentive for when she lost weight. I had a friend who did that—bought two of everything. It never made much sense to me, and as far as I knew, the smaller ones always ended up going to waste.

I sat on the bed with a slump and stared out the window.

I didn't know when it had begun to rain, but it had. The outside world looked fuzzy, white, like television static, bad reception.

I thought about Sophie's birthday party. It was beginning to blur with other moments that cluttered my memory. It didn't matter. The questions it posed were the same: Was it possible to fall out of love in a single moment? Possible for somebody to turn from lover to stranger in the glimpse of a smile? Maybe. I recalled a theory my father had concocted one night, while we sat in an Oakland juke joint sharing a plate of ribs. He'd said humor, above all else, was what bound each of us and separated each of us from one another. Humor was the great moment of truth. What we thought was funny was how we defined ourselves, and revealed ourselves, whether we knew it or not.

"So, yo, you want it or what?"

I sat up abruptly. Jiminy stood by the door holding a cell phone in his hands.

"'Cuz I gotta get goin'. My boy just paged me."

I hesitated, but not for long.

"Yes," I said, rising. "I'll take it."

Back at Andrew's apartment I packed my things in the living room while he stayed locked in his bedroom, listening to the same album he'd been listening to the night before. Every object appeared to me already as a memory of itself: The jazz albums stacked against the wall. A framed poster for a long-gone theater production of Tom Stoppard's *Travesties*. The humidifier by the window. The typewriter on his desk with his half-written play beside it.

On his refrigerator hung a black-and-white photograph strip of us. We had taken it months earlier in an old-fashioned photo booth—the kind that makes everybody look glamorous. I guess something about the way the ink settles, the high contrast it creates. We looked good. Not like ourselves but like movie stars who had been chosen to play us. In a drawer somewhere were a lot more of those same photos of Andrew and me. Our first few weeks together we'd been obsessive about getting them taken in the booth on Avenue B. At the end of every date, we'd end up back there, in that photo booth, staring into the darkened glass, waiting for the flash. As if we needed proof that we really existed.

In the strip he'd hung on the refrigerator, I am looking off to the side in each shot, frowning, as if there's some third party off-camera who is beckoning to me. Andrew is looking directly ahead into the lens, wearing a beatific smile.

When I was finished packing, I went and knocked on his door. I heard a bedspring creak, but he didn't answer.

"Andrew," I whispered. "Take care, okay?"

I waited for a reply, but there was nothing—just the grunge music playing its endless dirge.

I had the fleeting wish that there were two of me. I could leave one of them behind for him, a parting gift. Instead I left a check for half the rent on the kitchen table (he hadn't asked for it, but it felt cleaner that way), then let myself out.

MY FIRST NIGHT in the new place, I woke to the sound of a voice. It was three in the morning. The orchid sat beside me like a glowing white fist. Somebody was in the front of the apartment, weeping, raving. Around me, the bedroom was shrouded in a thick gray light. The voice was a woman's. Her muffled sobbing came to me from somewhere out there in the dark. I thought Vera had come home early from her travels. I scrambled out of bed, threw on my T-shirt, and stumbled down the hall, searching for the source. Only when I reached the living room and found it empty did I realize that the sound was not coming from my apartment at all, but rather from outside, on the street. I peered out and saw a woman ranting to herself at the subway station a half a block away. She was thin and dark, and her pregnant belly poked out like a tumor. She staggered around, clutching her hair, and yet the weeping had an aura of theater—like an echo of something real—the way drugged-out emotions sometimes do. I watched her until she had staggered off down the street and out of sight.

Afterward, I was restless. There were still a few hours until I could sanely leave for work. So I filled up the bathtub and lit the votive candles before stepping into the hot, bubbly water, wincing as it scalded my toes. I submerged myself slowly, and after a while my body adjusted, and the temperature grew comfortable. There in the candlelight I stared at my body. I took note of its features like a doctor examining a patient for the first time: broad shoulders, narrow hips, teardrop breasts that didn't quite match. One breast was small, prepubescent, with a pale pink nipple, the other slightly fuller, with a deeper mauve nipple. Like they belonged to two different women. I ran a hand across my mismatched breasts, then down across my belly, my thighs, and through the dark hair between my legs. I felt a surge of pity for this body—as if it were something separate from myself rather than something I lived inside. I pitied it as if it were a child I had just taken a dangerous toy away from, to spare it some potentially lethal accident. *It's for your own good. Someday you'll see.* I lay there thinking such thoughts until the water turned cold, and I was shivering, and it was really morning.

7

RETA HICKS WAITED FOR ME just beyond the revolving doors. I watched her for a moment from the lobby. She wore an old brown wool coat that had pilled up from use, and on her feet a pair of sneakers. Twisted around her wrist was a drugstore bag that held her work shoes—a pair of black low-heeled pumps, visible through the plastic. She stood with her back to me, and the smoke from her cigarette twirled up from her head, like steam from a spout.

This had been my idea. I was taking her out to dinner, a small token of appreciation for her having found me the apartment. But now I wasn't sure I had it in me. A stranger. A night of polite conversation. I considered making up an excuse: I was coming down with a cold, would she take a rain check?

"Greta," I said, stepping out into the cold.

She turned, smiling, bluish gray smoke leaking out of her nose and mouth.

She looked different. It must have been the makeup. She wore a color scheme from another era. Slashes of pink blush, pearlescent coral lipstick. Her eyes were decorated with sparkly blue eye shadow.

She flung her cigarette into the gutter and smiled widely. "There she is. Working late?"

"Yeah, sorry. I lost track of time."

"That's okay. I'm just glad you're here now."

I opened my mouth to tell her I couldn't do it tonight, but the combination of her eager smile and the heavy makeup made me change my mind.

I brought her to Le Zoo, a French bistro five blocks south of the office, where the publisher had taken me my first week on the job—apparently a Riggs Fellow tradition. Then I'd been too nervous to taste the steak frites and flourless chocolate cake he'd treated me to, and I'd always wanted to come back.

The maître d' took our coats. Beneath hers Greta was all gussied up: a midnight blue silk blouse, a white polyester skirt and matching blazer. A cloud of gardenia perfume surrounded her and now me. On her ears, tiny diamonds glinted. She'd made a real effort. I was glad I hadn't canceled.

She did most of the talking over dinner—a steady stream of gossip about our fellow workers. In her short time at the magazine, she'd learned everybody's business. She told me which editor was vying to take over the helm. Which one was alcoholic. Which was divorced and dating a woman half his age. Which overweight food critic had been caught having sex in her office late one night with a certain chatty Latino mailman.

I half listened. All around us were older men in suits, red-faced, corpulent. My eyes settled on a young man across the room—a thin blond waiter who reminded me a bit of Andrew. He was reciting the specials to a geriatric couple, who stared up at him with rheumy eyes. His cheeks flushed the way Andrew's did when he was embarrassed or too warm.

Out of the corner of my eye, I could see Greta making a gagging gesture with her finger in her mouth. She was imitating somebody. She was telling a story. I'd missed the beginning. She pulled her finger out of her mouth and wiped it on a napkin. "Well, she sure didn't get that skinny by dieting."

I tried to sound as if I'd been listening. "Oh, really?"

"Really really," she said, and took a gulp of wine. I saw she'd almost finished the bottle.

She leaned forward, her elbows on the table. "How are you holding up?"

In her eyes brewed sympathy and hunger. She wanted to play big sister.

"I'm fine," I told her.

"Honest?" She stared at me with a sort of jutting intensity.

"Yeah, honest."

The truth was, just that morning I had woken up unable to move. My eyes had blinked open, but my body was as if paralyzed. I lay completely still in that other girl's stark bedroom for what had to be ten minutes. I sent my body messages from my brain, but it didn't hear them. I tried to speak, but my voice muscles weren't listening either. And then, after what seemed an eternity, my body jerked into gear like a car engine finally catching, and I lay there gasping, as if I'd been held under water.

Greta was still watching me.

I cocked my head and put on my best reporter's voice. "So tell me about yourself, Greta. Who are you?"

It worked. People always preferred to talk about themselves. "Ah," she said. "The forty-thousand-dollar question. Well, for starters," she said, "I don't look like what I am." She went on to explain that she was the daughter of a German woman and a black GI. Her father had, she said, liberated the Jews from Buchenwald in World War II. Her mother had lived in a village on the outskirts of the camp, and he'd liberated her, too, in a way.

As she spoke, I laughed inwardly at the coincidence. It was funny. I hadn't noticed it before, but now that she'd said it, I could see it—what we had in common. In fact, we bore a slight resemblance to each other. Nothing obvious, but yes, we could have been related. We had the same straight brown hair and olive skin, and the same vague look about our features.

"I grew up on army bases all over the world," she was saying. "Seoul. Bombay. Frankfurt. San Diego. And Kenya. I'm a regular United Nations. I always tell people I'm from Nowhere, Everywhere. It's the only honest answer. You know?"

I nodded, though I didn't know.

"And what about you?" She was watching me, smiling, waiting for me to reciprocate. I wondered if she already knew my story. I doubted it. Nobody ever knew before I told them. Except Lola. She'd known from the first time she saw me at the Black Student Union meeting our freshman year. I'd stood awkwardly in the back, hands shoved in my pockets, pretending not to notice the whispers and stares. Lola walked across the room, stood in front of me, arms akimbo. I thought she was going to ask me to leave, but then she smiled slowly and said, "Hey, are you *nusu-nusu*?" For a moment I thought she was mistaking me for somebody else, a girl named Nusu-Nusu. But she went on to explain. She was studying Swahili. It was the word for girls like me. Literal translation: *partly-partly.*

I told Greta now. The words felt slightly stale. I'd had to say them so many times.

"So you see," I said when I finished. "We have something in common."

She laughed, shaking her head, "Yes, we do!"

I still couldn't tell whether my story had come as a surprise to her or not. Did it matter? According to my parents, none of this was supposed to matter, these quirks of DNA. They were not supposed to change anything. But they did. As soon as Greta had told me, I'd felt an invisible wall fall away between us.

We ordered dessert, flourless chocolate cake for me, crème brûlée for her. I suggested we get brandies as well.

"So what happened with that boy of yours?" she asked me. "Why'd you move out in such a rush?"

I paused, then told her the whole story, my eyes turned down. "I suppose I should have been more—forthright, but—"

"But you wanted to just be yourself. Without all that other stuff mucking it up."

Had that been it? I nodded, trying to decide.

"Well, it wouldn't have made a difference," she said. "He would have just hidden his true colors, played Mr. Sensitive for a while, Mr. Curious, Mr. Enlightened, and then one night, when you were in real deep, he'd let his real self slip out." A hint of anger had crept into her voice. "At least this way everything came out at the start."

I nodded. It made sense what she was saying.

"I say hurrah to you for walking away." Greta lifted her glass of brandy and swished the brown liqueur from side to side. "Learn your lessons early and you'll save yourself a lot of bullshit down the line."

We clinked glasses and she leaned forward then, a mischievous smile playing on her lips. "You know what? I think we should start our own nation. If only we had some loot. We could buy an island—one of those little Tahitian joints that Marlon Brando got himself. And we could fill it with people just like us. And never have to deal with the bullshit again."

I laughed. "Now there's an idea."

"I'll be the minister of defense."

"And I'll be the minister of information. We can wear suits and bow ties like those Fruit of Islam men. And sell bean pies to passing sailors."

"It'll be splendid!" She closed her eyes and began to recite, haltingly: *"In Xanadu did Kubla Khan, A stately pleasure-dome decree: Where Alph, the sacred river, ran, Through caverns measureless to man, Down to a sunless sea. . . ."*

I watched her face as she went on with the poem. She had a lot of potential, underneath the gaudy makeup and the extra ten pounds. But there was something dusty about her looks, tarnished, like something that's been put to use one too many times. She seemed lonely to me. She wore no wedding ring, and I wondered if she had given up on love, or if she had someone at home, a warm body in the dark.

"So twice five miles of fertile ground, With walls and towers were girdled round . . ."

She opened her eyes and broke into a bashful smile. "Like that. It'll be like that."

OUTSIDE, the temperature had dropped. It hurt to breathe in too deeply. I waited while Greta hailed herself a cab, and felt a slight dread at the thought of Vera's cold white bedroom awaiting me at the other end of my trip.

Greta spoke with her back to me, her arm held up toward traffic. "Thank you for the dinner. The whole evening, really. You didn't have to."

"But I wanted to. It was the least I could do. You got me out of a real bind."

A cab with its vacant lights on pulled up in front of her. She stepped off the curb. "So we'll do it again?"

"Yes, I'd like that," I said, realizing only as I said it that it was true.

She opended the door, but paused, and turned to smile at me through a web of rain. "You know, you're never really alone. Not really."

I looked down and kicked the pavement. I hadn't known I was that obvious. "I'm fine—" I began, but when I looked up she had already slipped inside the cab.

WHEN I GOT BACK to the apartment that night, I was overwhelmed by the smell. A perfume so strong it had outlasted the girl herself. I cracked open the living room window, but other smells wafted inside: marinated chicken wings and marijuana. I left it open anyway and went to the kitchen and began making some tea, but when I stopped moving for a moment, I heard from behind the stove a distinct scratching sound and a slight squeaking. I recalled the glue traps Andrew had used in his apartment. Recalled him pulling out the remains of one mouse that had gotten stuck—a tiny dust-colored creature with its buckteeth glued to the trap. I listened now, terrified, to the scratching noise, imagining every time it moved it only becoming more enmeshed in the stickiness.

When I went to the bedroom, I saw there was a message blinking on the answering machine. I felt a lurch of hope, despite myself, that it was Andrew. But he didn't have my number. And when I pressed play, an older man's voice—he said his name was Tony, he had a thick Brooklyn accent—began speaking to Vera. A stream of obscenities.

"Yo, Vera, how's that juicy pussy of yours doin'? I've been thinkin' about it. Been thinkin' about fuckin' you every night. You and your big bouncing titties."

The talk went on for a minute and I listened, cheeks flaming, until his voice—jerky, aroused—was finally cut off by the tape. I pressed erase and stood over the machine, breathing tightly for a moment.

I looked around the room. I felt all of a sudden homesick. I lay on the bed, staring at the sole photograph I'd brought with me from California. It was an old snapshot with white scalloped edges. I couldn't tell the date or how old I'd been when it was taken, but my father wore an Afro, and the lapels on his shirt suggested the seventies. In the picture, my brother and I were dressed alike: blue bell-bottoms and rainbow-striped polyester shirts. I hadn't noticed it before now, but my brother looked a little cross-eyed in the picture, as if he were trying to see in two directions at once. And my left hand was twisted in my lap in such a way that it appeared deformed.

I tossed the picture onto my night table. The last time I'd seen them all in person was June, my graduation. Class of 1992. After the ceremonies we'd gone out to celebrate at El Torito, a Mexican restaurant in the center of Palo Alto. My father wore a white smock and shoveled corn chips into his mouth as if he were afraid they'd be snatched away. My mother, blond and thin and dressed in a Maoist peasant jacket, sent the waiter back with her food twice to remove first the cheese, then the tortilla itself from her burrito, explaining she was allergic to wheat and dairy. My brother and his girlfriend wore matching sun-baked dreadlocks. They squirmed and tore at their clothes like a couple of mermaids who could not breathe outside water. They didn't stop their wiggling until they excused themselves to take some hits from a joint. They came back fifteen minutes later, red-eyed and smirking. As usual, I played the stiff, making apologetic faces at the waiters and throwing nervous glances at the bourgeois families celebrating their own children's graduations around us.

At some point I passed around a copy of the magazine where I would be working. My parents were politely silent, but my brother flipped through it for a few minutes, looked up, and said, "Do people still read this shit?"

Then they all laughed, a little too hard, as if this was the funniest thing in the world.

These days they were all unreachable. My father was on sabbatical, traveling around the Middle East for six months, part of his requisite pilgrimage to Mecca. I had received a few postcards from him along the way—from the Gulf of Oman and Egypt—saying *"As-salaam alaikum"* and telling me how beautiful the people in this or that region were. My mother was on a prolonged silent meditation at a Zen retreat in Northern California. And my brother was a champion surfer who was at this very moment chasing waves around the world with his girl. He had sent me one postcard from Haleiwa, written in incomprehensible surfspeak.

It felt to me that they were always laughing at me across a dinner table. My parents had divorced long ago, but it had been an almost imperceptible rupture. To this day they remained living in the same house, my father on one floor, my mother on the other. They often ate dinner together in front of the news, barking out enraged commentary on the latest government corruption. They shared the same politics and the same sense of humor, and very occasionally one of them would go out on a date with somebody else, only to come home early, rolling their eyes, making wisecracks to the other about the poor sod or broad with whom they'd spent the miserable evening. They liked to say they had never broken up; they had simply evolved to a higher plane of friendship.

My father had left me with no way to reach him in Mecca, but my mother had given me the number of the Zen center where she was staying. "In case of emergency," she'd said, slipping the paper into my hand at the airport, smiling as if she knew there would be no such thing. I called it now.

An irritated man answered on the fifth ring.

I asked for her by name.

"And who's calling?"

"Her daughter."

"Is this an emergency?"

I hesitated. I could not honestly say it was an emergency. "No. I just, well, I just wanted to talk to her." I laughed. Buddhists made me nervous. "I guess I'm just a little homesick."

His tone shifted then. He sighed, and through the phone wires I could almost feel him trying to control his temper. His voice, when he spoke, was clipped, nasal, irate. "I'm not sure if your mother explained to you what goes on here, but she's on a silent retreat. Three months of no talking. So unless it's urgent, I'm going to have to take a message for her on paper, which I will put in her cubbyhole tomorrow."

"Okay—"

"But I'll be honest with you. Any kind of invasion from the outside can be disruptive to the process. So unless it's absolutely necessary—"

"Can't she talk to me for five minutes? What harm could that really do? Then I won't call again. I promise. Not until she's finished."

"Finished? What exactly do you mean, finished? This is a process that doesn't end."

I swallowed. I could hear the man's breathing. Smooth, calm, metered.

"I'm sorry," I said in a tiny voice. "Never mind. It doesn't matter."

I FELL ASLEEP that night with my clothes on.

In the dream Vera had returned home from her travels to find me asleep in her bed. She crawled in beside me. A big-boned white girl with blind, baby eyes and a scratchy Janis Joplin voice, she held one hand loosely around my neck while the other circled my areola. She whispered that she was going to kill me, but first she had to make me come. I wanted to stop her, but I was paralyzed. Leaden. Only my eyes were working as she slithered down under the sheets and I felt her tongue working between my legs. I came without wanting to, without moving, invisible shudders. When I woke up, there was a stickiness in the space between. The room was shrouded in a thick blue light. The smell was everywhere. In the sheets. The pillows. The surface of my skin.

8

LUCKY GIRL!" said Donna, the secretary, when she passed me in the hall the next morning.

I was on my way back from an ideas meeting on the fourteenth floor.

"Lucky how?" I said, but she just winked and kept walking.

I hesitated when I got to the door of my office. On my desk sat a huge bouquet of long-stemmed yellow roses. I approached them warily. My throat closed. I picked up the attached note and opened it.

The card said simply, "Without you I am nothing."

I stared at the words. *God, Andrew,* I thought, *get a grip.* But my body reacted with a mind of its own—a heave in my chest, like an aborted sob, and then slight dizziness.

When I found my balance, I crumpled the card and tossed it in the trash. I started to throw out the roses, too, but stopped. They were too beautiful to discard. It seemed criminal. I marched down the hall with the bouquet. I passed Donna along the way. Heard her call out, "So who's Romeo?" But I didn't answer. I just kept walking toward the red glowing sign marked EXIT. I ran down the stairwell two flights and came out the metal door onto the business floor.

I found Greta sitting in a wide-open corral with the other

fact-checkers. She was pouring a packet of Equal into a McDonald's cup and flipping through a magazine. Her cubicle, I saw, was a mess. Papers stacked in tilting sculptures. Books pilfered from the review-copy room in a heap at her feet. She had *Cathy* cartoons stuck in the corkboard over her desk, along with a postcard of an orangutan dressed in a hard hat and overalls.

I stopped a few feet away from her desk, and just observed her for a moment, not speaking. A feeling rose up in me, both sick and sad. The office air, the fluorescent lights—I wanted to be outside, far away.

She looked up and blinked, surprised, I guess, to see me there.

"Hey—"

I dropped the bouquet onto her desk. "I just got these from my ex-boyfriend. I thought you might want them. I just can't have them around."

She touched her chest. "God, they're stunning. Are you sure?"

I nodded.

She picked them up slowly. "These must have cost a fortune." She frowned at me, deep furrows between her eyebrows. "This seems wrong. Me taking them. Can't we at least split them?"

"No. I really don't want them anywhere near me."

She saw something on my face. "Oh, geez, hon. It kills me to see you hurting this way. I wish there was something I could do."

I managed a smile. "You've already helped," I said. "Enjoy the flowers."

I did not hear from Andrew after that. The phone in the apartment rang sometimes late at night, but nobody had my number there, so it was never for me.

"Hey, sugar, what you wearin'?"

The voice was baritone. An older black man. The clock read 2:38 a.m. In the invisible background, I could hear Luther Vandross singing "Creeping."

I told the man, groggily, that I wasn't Vera, that I was a subletter.

"Yeah, right. And I'm Harry Belafonte." He paused, inhaled something. Spoke in a high, tight voice. "You wearing a thong?"

I insisted that I was somebody else.

"Come on, sugar. Talk to me like you did last time. Get on your hands and knees and—"

"I'm not Vera."

"For real?"

"For real."

"Where the hell is she?"

"London."

"Shit. Tell her Sammy called," he said, and hung up.

9

YOU'VE GOT A LOT of potential," Greta said. "But your colors, they're all wrong."

We were underground, at Rockefeller Center station. It was evening. I'd spent all day trekking around Central Park, trying to interview mothers about new high-tech playground designs. But all the women were brown, and the children were white, and none of them were related. I'd interviewed the women anyway, but when I handed the piece in, my editor, Rula Maven, said it wouldn't work. We couldn't quote the nannies.

Greta's uptown train was on the other platform, but she had insisted on coming with me to mine so she could finish convincing me that I needed this service. Color analysis. Something I recalled vaguely from the 1980s—a fad that had come and gone with the mullet.

"See, everybody has a season," Greta was saying beside me. "Autumn, Winter, Spring, or, blech, Summer. I'm a Winter. Deep Winter. And just knowing that has changed my life. I kid you not."

Near us, a person in a wheelchair was begging for change. At first I'd thought it was a runaway teenaged boy, all croaky voice and motherless smile. But now, on second glance, it looked more like an old woman, her wiry body wasted by drugs and alcohol and maybe disease. I couldn't say for sure. It was dressed in layers: a grimy green parka over an "I Love New York" sweatshirt. Its face was hidden behind the bill of a Redskins baseball cap.

"I know just the woman to take you to," Greta was saying. "For fifty bucks, she does an analysis. Want to try it? We could go some afternoon."

The person in the wheelchair was raising its eyes to grin at us. The person's skin looked strange, as if it was stretched too tightly, like it might rip if he or she smiled any harder.

I looked back at Greta. "Fifty bucks. That's a little steep. And anyway, wouldn't I be the same as you? I mean, color-wise?"

"Not necessarily. It's a science. You have to get a degree to diagnose people. That's why I want to take you to this woman. She's studied in Europe. She's a genius. I'm telling you."

The person was moving toward us, Big Gulp cup outstretched. I stared hard into its face, trying to decide once and for all. Boy, girl, old man, or old woman. No clue. Even the voice was unclear. A raspy wail as it sang out its plea. *Wheelchair basketball, wheelchair basketball. Wouldn't you like to give to wheelchair basketball?*

I could hear a rumble in the distance, the train approaching. Greta frowned at the wheelchair person for the first time, just noticing it, and turned away from its outstretched cup to face me.

"Anyway," Greta said, stepping closer to me. "What do you say? The colors. This weekend?"

The person was waiting, looking at me now for change. I

fumbled in my pocket and tossed some silver into its cup. It wheeled off to the next person.

"Well, it's kind of out of my price range—"

"Oh, come on. How much is your happiness worth?"

My train rolled into the station just then. "All right, all right, maybe I'll give it a try."

"That's a girl."

I pushed my way into the subway car with the rest of the passengers and turned back to look at *it* for one more guess. But *it* had disappeared.

Greta was still there. She smiled and waved and mouthed: *This weekend?*

I hesitated, then nodded, because it was silly. I had no other plans. This wasn't what I'd imagined for my grown-up life in New York—going to color analysis with a woman twice my age. But for now this was all I had—and she was growing on me, in her own funny way.

I WAS a Winter, usually too.

Greta sat on a stool in a corner of the woman's apartment, holding her coat on her lap, smiling broadly with vicarious pleasure as the woman draped one polyester cloth after another before my face.

"Oh, yes, you're a deep Winter," the woman cooed. "This here? Lobelia? This is your ball-gown color." She clucked her teeth at me in the mirror. "Gorgeous."

I stared at my reflection. I looked like somebody's child with the purple swatch tucked like a bib into my shirt.

The woman—Dorothea was her name—told me she was

a Spring. She had ashen blond hair and pinkish skin with, she pointed out, blue undertones. She appeared to be in her mid-fifties. She wore a chartreuse green blouse under a black polyester pants suit, and gold earrings. On her lip was a giant, blooming herpes sore. It glistened with the ointment she'd put on it.

"Now, you should never wear gold," she said, crinkling her nose as she held a metallic gold cloth up to my face. "See that? Cheap. A Winter always looks more expensive in silver."

Her apartment was a dark and cluttered fourth-floor walk-up in the Village. It served as both her home and her color studio.

"I live and breathe color," she'd said when we came inside, pointing to an entire shelf filled with books covering every angle of the subject—from a large, glossy photo book of Tuscan pottery to the bible of her trade, *The Elements of Color,* by Johannes Itten of the Bauhaus School in Germany, where Dorothea said she had studied.

Signed headshots of actors were plastered along one wall. They'd apparently all come seeking color advice. None was famous, as far as I could tell. One of the faces—a ruddy white man in his fifties who in the photo posed in a construction worker's uniform—did strike me as familiar, and while Dorothea talked about the perils of greens and yellows on a girl of my complexion, I remembered where I'd seen him before. He was the M&M Man. I'd watched him in commercials as a child. I could still see his big hand opening to reveal the clutter of multicolored candies to the lot of greedy children.

"You're the only season who can get away with wearing black and white together," Dorothea said, holding both colors up to my face. "See? Gorgeous," she said. "Now somebody like me, a Spring, can't get away with it. The contrast is too harsh." She scowled at herself in the mirror as she held the black and white swatches side by side up to her own face. "I look cheap," she said. "Like a caterer."

Just then, from the abyss of the apartment, a teenage boy wandered into the living room, yawning. He was blond, lanky, with braces and acne, and wore a faded gray T-shirt and boxer shorts. He looked half asleep, but jerked awake at the sound of Dorothea's voice.

"Goddammit, Ricky!" she shrieked at the sight of him. "Can't you see? I'm working!" Her cheeks had reddened in embarrassment or maybe rage. I couldn't tell.

He blinked awake and scratched his hair and muttered, "Sorry, I just wanted some juice," before turning around and shrinking back down the hall again.

She winced a smile at me. "Excuse me a minute." Then, in clicking high heels, she followed him into the darkened hallway.

I could hear the sound of her whisper as she scolded the boy. I caught the words "asinine" and "privacy" and "a business, for God's sake." Something fell to the floor and smashed.

"Pretty cool stuff, huh?" Greta whispered to me from her perch on the stool.

I thought the whole thing was pretty ridiculous, but I didn't say anything. I didn't want to offend Greta. We sat there for what seemed a good while waiting for Dorothea to return. All had gone quiet down the hall. I was hot and bored and still had a puke yellow bib on—something Dorothea had put on me to show me a wrong color. Greta was still watching me. I tried to make a joke and pointed at the gallery of headshots. "Do you think Dorothea autographed them all herself?"

Greta didn't laugh. Her mouth tightened into a straight line and her eyes drifted behind me. I turned. Dorothea stood in the doorway watching us. She had her hands on her hips. I couldn't tell if she had heard me. She sniffed and crossed the floor. "I'm sorry about the interruption. It won't happen again."

Somewhere, deep down the hall, I heard her son sobbing. Dorothea went and turned on the stereo to classical music and cleared her throat.

"Now, where was I?" she asked, her voice still tense with what had gone on in the other room.

The next twenty minutes were a blur: rules spat at me from thin red lips, swatches flying, wrist flicking makeup onto my face. Then, for forty dollars extra, she offered to do an analysis of my "clothing personality." I was either *dramatic*, *gamine*, *romantic*, *ingénue*, or *classic*—but she wouldn't tell me which until I gave her the forty dollars. I declined the service but lied and promised to come back soon when I had some extra money.

At the door, she handed me my wallet of color swatches, which she told me I should always carry with me in my purse for reference.

"Eventually, you won't need it. But for now, the first few years, you really need to refer to it when shopping."

Greta piped in beside me, "I never leave home without mine."

Dorothea reached out to shake my hand. "Well, it's awfully nice to lay eyes on you. Greta told me about you over the summer. She kept saying, 'Wait'll you see this friend of mine. She's just like me.' She was in such a state about it."

I looked at Greta. She had her eyes fixed on Dorothea. She wore a stiff smile.

I was silent as we went down the stairs. I could hear voices behind Dorothea's door—the teenage boy sobbing enraged epithets—*bitch, cunt, I hate you*—at his mother.

Outside, a soft rain fell. I stood under the awning beside Greta while she fumbled in her purse and pulled out a pack of cigarettes.

"That was funny," I said. "What Dorothea said? This summer? We barely knew each other."

Greta paused. I saw, under the beige of her skin, that she was blushing. She looked away at the street, then back at me. "I know. But I felt like I knew you. I just, well, I had this feeling we'd be friends."

She looked so flustered that I had to laugh.

"It's okay." I shook my head. "I just got a little confused, that's all."

She bit her lip and searched my face. "Are you mad?"

I shook my head. "Oh, please. Not at all." Because I wasn't. I touched her arm. "Really. It's no biggie. Hey, I'm glad we're friends. I'm glad your prediction came true!"

Greta grinned, visibly relieved. "Now tell me what you thought. She's a genius, right?"

I started to tell her what I really thought—but changed my mind. I humored her. "Yeah, you were right. It was worth it."

"And now you'll see," Greta said, turning to face the street. "The world is made up of people wearing the wrong colors. Except you and me, of course."

She linked her arm in mine. "So. Tell me. Do you like hot wings? 'Cause there's a bar near here. Houlihan's. They have Happy Hour every night from five-thirty to seven-thirty. Two for one on drinks. Even on the weekends. And they serve hot wings half price. Fries too. But I try to resist the fries." She patted her hip. "Urban sprawl. At my age, you gotta be careful."

And the next thing I knew the two of us were running through the rain, laughing together under her Chase Manhattan umbrella.

HOULIHAN'S WAS PACKED—a dingy sports bar with Budweiser and Heineken mirrors lining the walls. Guns N' Roses played from the jukebox. There were a million and one clean and stylish bars in the Village, but Greta had chosen this. Still, I was glad not to be going home just yet to my stinky apartment. While she ran off to get us our drinks, I saved a booth in the back.

A few tables away sat a couple. I watched them while I waited. The girl was thin, her feathered hair tinted a silvery blond. The man wore a suit and glittery cuff links, his light brown hair gelled back. Their skin was an identical bronze—a raceless shade of brown I imagined they'd achieved during a recent vacation to Club Med in Cancún or maybe Aruba.

I thought about Andrew. I tried to imagine him and his friends in a place like this. He preferred down-and-out dives on the Lower East Side, the tempered debauchery of junkies and those who just looked like junkies. He had an aversion to this world of productive, white-collar, Midtown professionals. He was funny that way. He fancied himself a workingman's writer, but his background flared up in certain moments, making its presence known, like malaria emerging from remission.

I recalled one night, toward the beginning of our relationship, when we lay together in the dark, planning a trip across the country. Some part of me had known even then that we would never take it, but I had indulged the fantasy anyway, suggesting we get a sleeper car on an Amtrak train. But Andrew didn't like the idea. He wanted to take a Greyhound bus. He said he loathed Amtrak. The people on Amtrak, he'd said, were the bane of American culture. I hadn't known exactly what he was talking about at the time—which people?—but sitting here, in Houlihan's, I understood: it was the solid middle class. He, of Bendover, of Old Money, of trust funds, hated their bourgeois pretensions. It was the working class he found romantic—steel mill workers in Pittsburgh, trailer trash in New Hampshire, welfare mothers in Detroit. Drug addicts on the Lower East Side, even. These middling professionals with their forty-hour work weeks, their mundane aspirations, their Banana Republic shirts, their Coach purses, had set his teeth on edge.

That night he'd gone on to say that what he loved about me was that I was neither the sort to take a Greyhound nor the type to take an Amtrak. No, he'd said. I was the kind of girl who'd drive a 1974 powder blue Volvo sports coupe with sheepskin seat covers. The interior would smell of clove cigarettes and dust and car oil, and the floor would be a clutter of rumpled road maps and mix-tapes made by boyfriends gone by. "Yeah," he'd said, smiling at me through the darkness, his eyes filled with an intensity that made me both nervous and happy. "That's what you'd drive. Right out of town."

Of course he was wrong. I'd taken an Amtrak train several times with my family, and the womblike lull of a train in motion was my favorite form of transportation. You saw poor people riding side by side with rich flying-phobics. And everything in the middle. And it seemed on those journeys that the lines broke down. There was camaraderie among the riders, as if for those hours on the train, they were one.

But I hadn't contradicted Andrew, preferring to indulge his fantasy of me in a powder blue vintage car.

Greta came back carrying our drinks—a whiskey sour for me and a sidecar for herself, and an enormous pile of hot wings, glistening and orange. "I put some songs on the jukebox, too—though it may take a while for them to play."

I took my drink. "Thanks. How much?"

She shook her head. "It's on me. You can get the next round."

She took a hearty gulp of her drink, then started in on a chicken wing dipped in cool ranch sauce. I picked one off the pile and put it on my plate, but I was unable to actually eat it. It reminded me for some reason of the rodent in the glue trap I'd heard scraping around the other night at Vera's place. The squeaking had eventually stopped, but I'd been afraid to pull back the stove to throw away the remains.

Greta finished off a wing, smacked her lips, and tossed the bone onto her plate, and I only half listened as she began to chatter on about an affront to her that day at work. "So I go into his office and David Shapiro doesn't even look up at me, he just grunts out his request to me without even looking up from his lousy computer. . . ."

Behind Greta, I could see the Club Med couple engaged in a hot make-out session. I watched their tongues intertwine, wetly rotate around each other. Watched the man's hand creep up the woman's rib cage, rest just beneath her ample, Victoria's Secret–clad breast. I remembered a time not so long ago when Andrew and I had kissed like that at a subway station, late at night, after a movie. Him leaning against the grimy wall, his hands tucked into my back pockets, cupping my ass. That night, I'd closed my eyes and drifted away from the dank station and into our intimacy—until I heard a voice—female, young, brash—say, "Them motherfuckers need to take that shit home!" I'd pulled back from his embrace to see a group of teenage girls dressed in bomber jackets. They stood a few feet away from us. Varying shades of brown. They were eyeing us, laughing. "White ho!" one of them had shouted, then they all bolted down the platform, cackling at their own audacity. Andrew had watched them, too, smirking, unperturbed, and muttered, "Heifers," before trying to pull me back to his embrace. But I had pulled away, crossed my arms.

He had smiled tenderly at me. "You're not embarrassed now, are you?"

I'd just shaken my head and stepped away toward the edge of the platform, peered down the dark tunnel. "Come on, fucking train," I'd said under my breath, feeling desperate all of a sudden to get back to the secrecy of his apartment.

"Listen!" Greta said, jarring me out of my thoughts.

She was grinning, pointing to the air. "The song. It's one of my selections."

It was the Rolling Stones. "Wild Horses."

She closed her eyes and rocked her head and began to sing along.

After a few stanzas, she opened her eyes and smiled lazily. "This is the best line. Listen."

I listened. *Graceless lady, you know who I am.*

"What's so great about that line?"

She looked surprised. "Oh come on, what do you think?" Then she sang her version loudly, imitating Mick Jagger's slur: *Raceless lady, you know who I am.*

"Are you sure that's what he's saying?"

She nodded. "Yeah, that's what he's saying. You gotta listen more closely. This is our song, girl."

I listened. He said it again. *Graceless.* It was definitely *graceless.* I said, "You're wrong. Listen again."

He said the lyric one last time. *Graceless.*

She shook her head, and her eyes flashed, and for a minute I thought she was angry. "You're just not listening," she said, and closed her eyes and began to sing along loudly to the rest of the song.

I was glad when the music shifted to somebody else's selections—it was country, twangy. Greta rolled her eyes and grumbled, "Ugh, I hate this shit, don't you?"

I nodded quickly. "Yeah, I'm not a big country-western fan."

She gave me a crooked smile. "I didn't think so." She lifted her glass to me. "To sisterhood."

"To sisterhood," I repeated. We clinked glasses. Afterward, there was an awkward silence, and I tried to think of something funny to say but found myself speechless, as if we were strangers after all. We sat with our drinks and our cold hot wings, looking at everything but each other, and after a while I feigned a yawn and said I was beat and had better get home to bed.

10

HE SMELL of the apartment did not fade. And I noticed other ones beneath it. Smells of skin and hair and sweat in her sheets no matter how much I washed them, and the thick fetid odor of menstruation in the bathroom no matter how much I scrubbed the toilet. Smells of takeout meals in the kitchen. Underneath all these was a faint odor of chemicals, a smell that reminded me of my high school biology class when I dissected a frog. It was an experience I have never forgotten. When I sliced into the frog's belly I found it was pregnant—a clump of tiny eggs had stared up at me. The smell of formaldehyde had stayed with me, and I detected it here in the apartment, ever so faintly.

I got a few more obscene phone calls. One was a message on the machine, like the first one, the same gravelly voice talking in detail about Vera's genitalia.

Beyond Vera's suitors, I got calls from creditors wanting Vera to pay them the money she owed.

They always called in the evening, when I was just settling down in front of the news. Family time. Dinnertime. They were voices so nasal I imagined that was all they were: a series of giant noses calling me.

"Hello, is this Vera Cross?"

This one had called before. He was a gay nose, and I imagined him seated on the other end of the line, in a cubicle, surrounded by rows and rows of other noses—WASP noses, African noses, Jewish noses, Chinese noses, Puerto Rican noses—all speaking in one blur of nasal harassment.

He had called yesterday before dawn and demanded I pay the institution to which I owed money. I could not make out the institution's name. Something like Pippin and Grossberg. He had not believed me when I told him I was not Vera Cross.

"This is not Vera Cross," I said to him again tonight. "She went away. Try again next year."

But he didn't seem to hear me.

"I'm sorry to inform you that there's a lien on you."

As he went on naming the large sum of money I owed and what legal action would be taken against me should I fail to pay it, I drew the face with my finger in the fog on the windowpane. The woman I'd never grown tired of drawing.

He was chewing gum, swiftly and loudly. "Have you received our letters?"

"I'm sure I did. But I didn't open them. I put them in the closet, with the rest of Vera's mail. See, it's illegal to open mail that is not your own. And I'm not Vera. I don't know where she is or who she is."

He made a sound that made me understand the word *snicker*. "Okay, whatever you say. Have a great day, Vera."

I hung up the phone. The funny thing was, I didn't mind the calls. Or the mail, for that matter. They were reminders to me that my own life was not so bad after all. Or at least that it could get a whole lot worse.

AT HOULIHAN'S a few nights later I discussed Vera's money problems with Greta.

"See," I said, "I'm worried that she's gonna keep my deposit. Anybody this irresponsible with her finances—"

"Oh, I doubt that. And if Jiminy tries to stiff you, I will personally give you back every dime you lose. I would feel so responsible."

"Don't be ridiculous. You did me a favor, Greta. That doesn't mean you're responsible for what happens to me after that. God, I don't know what I would have done if you hadn't shown up when you did. I'm the one who owes you."

She looked pleased. "Well I'm just happy we're friends now. That's payment enough for me."

I smiled at her, but a fleeting, jagged thought—crazy and no doubt unfair—crossed my mind: That I was, indeed, spending all this time around Greta out of gratitude. That this was all a kind of prolonged thank-you dinner.

ONE EVENING as I came inside the foyer on my way home from work, I met a woman who lived in my building. She was tall, brown-skinned, and looked to be in her forties. She wore a colorful African dress and head wrap, and tennis shoes on her feet. In her arms, under plastic wrap, was a Bundt cake. She watched silently as I opened Vera's mailbox and pulled out a handful of bills.

"Howdy, you new in the building? I don't remember seeing you before—"

I paused. Jiminy had not told me whether I could be open about the living arrangement. I tried to keep it vague. "Um, I'm just house-sitting for a friend."

"Oh yeah? Which friend?"

She wore glasses—huge, plastic, pink frames with thick bifocal lenses that made her eyes look like fish floating in a tank. They were focused on the letters I held in my hand, addressed to Vera Cross.

A sneer, barely perceptible, flickered across her face. "Oh, are you a friend of Vera's?"

I hesitated, then shook my head. Decided to just tell the truth. "A friend of a friend of a friend. That sort of thing. She's traveling and, well, I'm taking care of her place. I've never even met her."

She put a hand on her hip. "Good," she said, glancing over her shoulder as if to make sure we were alone. "Keep it that way, honey. That bitch was nothing but trouble for the building. I was just saying to Corky the other day—you know Corky? Anyway, I was just saying to her, 'Ain't seen Vera around lately. Maybe somebody finally took out the trash.' "

She laughed after she said it, a mean, throaty chuckle—the kind women have been making about other women since the dawn of ages. I felt oddly protective of Vera.

She held out her hand. "I'm Flo," she said. Her hands were slippery and soft, and smelled of cocoa butter. "Now, if you ever need anything, just come knockin'! Apartment 3C. I'm sort of the unofficial super around here."

There was beeping on the street outside, and I looked to see a battered Toyota double-parked in front of the building. I couldn't see the driver's face, just a hand waving. "There's my ride." And she headed with her Bundt cake into the night.

I SNOOPED THAT NIGHT, feeling a little foolish as I moved around Vera's apartment like a sleuth, turning over objects, opening drawers. I just skimmed the surface, nothing truly invasive, trying to guess what she looked like based on what she'd left behind. I found a red cardigan folded in a drawer. It smelled strongly of the perfume that lingered in the rest of the apartment. I found a big yellow button that said in red letters "Ask me how I lost fifty pounds," in a box in the closet, on top of a stack of flyers advertising a diet pill. A New Year's resolution list from a year before scrawled on a Hello Kitty notepad. "Get to the gym at least three X a week. Quit my fucking job. Take cooking classes. Meditate. Go back to school. Stop calling R.D." She had left no photos behind except for a bleary Polaroid of an older black man lying in her bed, stark naked, arms behind his head, penis flaccid, grinning up at the camera.

As I sat down to television with my dinner of spaghetti with Ragú sauce, toasted wheat bread on the side, I envisioned Vera as a female version of Jiminy. A pudgy blond girl—a sort of burned-out Teena Marie. Somebody who had long ago left her race—finding momentary liberation in the arms of black men. Yes. I could see it. Something about the way Flo had said, *Maybe somebody finally took out the trash.*

After dinner, I pulled out of my wallet a slip of paper with Greta's phone number on it. Just a few days before, she'd given it to me and told me to call her at home sometime. I hadn't done it yet.

I didn't want to bother her. Simply because I didn't know anybody in the city didn't mean she didn't either.

But she had said it as if she meant it, so I did now, tentatively.

She picked up on the first ring, but sounded out of breath. In a high voice, she asked if she could call back in a few.

I hung up and wondered if I'd caught her in the middle of sex. Of course I had. But with whom? I still hadn't been able to figure her out—what kind of man she liked, even if she liked men at all. We saw each other every day, but that was the thing about work colleagues. You knew them only in the sexless fluorescent light of the office.

I didn't expect her to really call back in a few, but she did.

"Hey, babe," she said, smacking on gum. "What's shakin'?"

"It wasn't important. If this is a bad time—"

"No, no. I was just—well." She giggled. "This guy—we were canoodling when you called."

"Oh, well, please don't let me interrupt."

"You aren't. He's gone. Really. It was enough for one date."

"Are you sure? Because we can talk tomorrow—"

"Silly, don't worry. I wouldn't have picked up if I didn't want to talk. Now forget about my horn-dog neighbor. His breath smelled like a gerbil's cage. Honest to God. What's up with you?"

I laughed. "Well, it was just that I got to snooping and I wanted to tell you what I found."

I told her about the various objects I'd uncovered.

Greta chuckled. "She sounds like a character. Tell me more."

I began to move around the apartment with the cordless phone tucked in the crook of my neck, lifting objects and books and describing them to Greta. Together, we fantasized about Vera. I stuck to my theory that she looked like Teena Marie. But Greta got stuck on the idea that she looked like Vanity, the sloe-eyed lead singer from the eighties pop band Vanity Six. We were both cracking up by the time we said good night.

THE NEXT MORNING, I felt it in my throat. A raw pain when I tried to swallow. My joints felt like an old woman's, arthritic. Outside, the sky was bone white. A cold draft seeped in through the window by the bed.

I showered, dressed in layers, then trudged down the hall to the closet and opened the door. Just above the Macy's bag overflowing with Vera's bills hung my jacket. Thin, corduroy. Beside it hung a coat—something Vera had left behind. It was a big down thing, swollen and bulky. Once it had been black, but from wear or washing it had turned the color of pencil smudge. It was ugly, but it looked warm. Warmer than my corduroy jacket. I pulled it out. Tried it on. It fit. I wore it to work. No harm done, though it made me look like an armadillo.

When I got there, Greta was standing in the lobby, perusing the magazine rack. We took the elevator up together. She said I looked ashen, as if I were coming down with something. "But," she added, eyeing me up and down, "I'm glad to see you wearing a sensible winter coat. In a Winter color, I might add."

I almost told her it was Vera's, but hesitated. She might think I was a thief. "I picked it up secondhand. Pretty ugly, huh?"

"No, not at all," she said. "It makes you look tough, like a real New Yorker."

We were at her floor now. The doors slid open. "Now, I want you to go on up to your desk and have a seat and get settled and I'll be up in a few with some cold remedies."

"You don't have to do that."

"Shush. It's no problem. I'm the nurse on duty here. I've got a whole pharmacy in my desk drawer." She winked at me. "Now just do what I say, okay?"

I did, and indeed, five minutes later, she entered my office carrying a handful of vitamins and a steaming cup of orange-hibiscus tea.

11

VERA'S ORCHID DIED. I woke up one morning, and it was gone—a shriveled brown nub at the top of the green stalk. And outside it was winter. When had that happened? Christmas lights were strung up like a whore's undergarments along Flatbush Avenue. There was no snow yet, but the muted sunlight was metallic, dreary. I could not remember the last clear day.

Over the weeks that followed, my body continued to send me signals that I was coming down with something, a full-fledged winter flu. Achy bones. A mildly sore throat. Vague symptoms of a problem, but not enough to see a doctor. I continued to wear Vera's coat everywhere, though I was rarely outdoors for more than a few minutes. I lived either belowground or high above. I spent my time scurrying between extremes: from the damp, cavelike darkness of a train station to the artificial light of my office twelve stories above ground. The earth itself was temporary—something to rush over in hard-soled shoes on your way to the next level.

I didn't spend much time at home either. I treated Vera's apartment as a trucker's rest stop: somewhere to shower, brush my teeth, change clothes. My sleep there felt like an eight-hour nap. There was nothing wrong with the place per se. Everything worked fine. There had been no trouble from

Jiminy. But when I was there, I felt ill. My symptoms were mild and vague. They roamed my body, like tinkers searching for new temporary homes where they could not be caught. Nausea one day, a dull ache behind my eyes the next. A rash on my neck like something crawling just beneath my skin.

The creditors continued their phone-harassment campaign, undeterred, but Vera's boyfriends stopped calling.

At the office, I worked hard, on articles of negligible importance. One week I wrote about the plight of big dogs living in cramped city apartments. It was apparently all the rage that year in New York to own a big dog in a tiny apartment—a Weimaraner if you were wealthy, a Rottweiler if you weren't. Rula Maven loathed pets ever since she'd stepped in a pile of fresh Great Dane feces on Park Avenue, wearing three-inch stilettos. She wanted me to show how the trend was cruel to animals.

But the dog psychologist I interviewed—a big-boned WASP with invisible lips and silver hair—said that despite what humans might think, dogs, big and small, actually prefer confinement to open spaces. "It's called the denning instinct," the woman told me flatly, staring into her own dog's kennel, where it lay sleeping so peacefully it looked dead to me. "They prefer rules and order over chaos," the psychologist insisted.

"It's a mistake to think the happiest dogs are country dogs, roaming the woods all day," she said. "The happiest dogs live in cages for most of their lives and are allowed outside only at regular intervals, to pee and defecate and exercise in fenced-in spaces."

I made a few halfhearted efforts to befriend my work peers. I went out for coffee with a wan brunette named Laurel who worked on the local desk. She told me within minutes of sitting down that she was having an affair with a married man. She spent our whole hour together shredding napkins with trembling fingers and spewing vitriol about his wife, whose fault it was that they couldn't see each other more often. "The marriage was already shit when I met him," she explained. "Their sex life was nonexistent. She was always depressed, suspicious. He's just being nice, sticking with it for the kids." I nodded and went home early.

Another night I went out for a drink after work with a reporter named Ross, who'd come from Mississippi and had started working at the magazine the same time as me. He amused me for a while with stories about his Baptist pediatrician father, but at some point switched to the subject of quotas. He said that if only he had been born in a different skin, he might be editor in chief of the magazine by now. And you, he said, if you were born black, who knows where you'd be? I was quiet while he ranted, and stared at my own face in the mirror behind the bar. My skin looked sallow, my eyes ringed by dark circles. Beside me, he was talking about how he wished he had come of age in the 1950s. Didn't I wish that, too? Because that was the golden age for people like us. I didn't answer, just kept staring at myself. *This is what they see when they look at you.* My eyes looked slightly stricken, and there was an ironic twist to my smile that seemed new to me—an expression I had acquired since graduation.

I didn't go out with Ross again after that. I didn't go out with Laurel, either. Both extended invitations, but I declined. I preferred Greta's company, even though she was twice my age and not on the same track as I was at work. Our friendship was—I'd decided—more than a thank-you dinner. She was the only work colleague I could stand to be around on a social basis. She was always available when I wanted to tie one on, and she was always sympathetic—no, empathetic—to my every grumble and complaint. She agreed with everything I said, and we spent many hours comparing our experiences of being "optical illusions," as she called us. When I wasn't working, I was with her, at Houlihan's, gnawing on chicken wings, putting back tumblers of scotch, and listening to her talk trash about our coworkers. She played "Wild Horses" every time. I'd stopped arguing with her about the lyrics. They were whatever she wanted them to be.

Sometimes it felt as if we'd known each other a lot longer than we had—as if she had in fact always been there, in my life, hovering beside me, a dotty spinster aunt. But other times it felt like no time at all—I knew so little about her life outside of work. Our friendship reminded me a little of a relationship I'd had with an older woman I'd worked with when I was in high school. Divina. She was a cashier at Ralph's supermarket on Shattuck. I was a bagger that summer, trying to save enough money for a senior trip to Catalina Island. Divina and I spent our breaks together every afternoon, seated in the park across from the store, me drinking a smoothie while Divina chain-smoked and complained to me about her life. She was slightly overweight, coiffed and perfumed. Pedicured and exfoliated. All breasts and ass. Her shoes always matched her belt, and she smoked cigarettes from a long brown filter. We had nothing in common except the place we worked, but we came to know each other in that oddly intimate way of coworkers. The fact that she was so much older than me, but not quite my parents' generation, made her feel like a safe respite from the brutal social politics of high school. Our time together felt slightly unreal, without consequence, and therefore peaceful. I relaxed in her presence. After high school graduation I quit my job and never saw her again.

I wondered if my friendship with Greta would last when the fellowship was over. How deep was it? I couldn't say. Only that she was always there for me, steady and comforting, wondering about my health, my welfare, my colors. On those nights when we didn't go to Houlihan's, she would call before bed to make sure I'd gotten home okay. And if she didn't, I would call her, just to speak to somebody. And she was always there to pick up on the first ring.

12

LOLA DID NOT write again. But one evening while I was working late at the office, I picked up the phone to hear a crackling international connection.

"Hey, baby."

I closed my eyes, surprised at how relieved I was to hear the sound of my father's soft Southern drawl.

He'd been to Mecca. Now he was staying in Cairo with friends—a couple named Zaid and Aisha. He was going to spend the next month or two sleeping in their guest room and working on an essay. He'd been having a wonderful experience on his sabbatical.

"And," he said, "I've gotten to know Zaid's son. A very handsome young man. Mustaffa. He's seen your picture." Behind him I heard a voice, thick and male and foreign. My father giggled like a schoolgirl. "He thinks you look Egyptian. He wants to know when you're coming to visit."

I rolled my eyes. "That's nice."

"He's about six-foot-one, broad shoulders, twenty-eight, a graduate student in engineering—"

"What is this? Some kind of marriage service? Don't you want to know how I'm doing?"

He sounded hurt. "Of course, baby, I was just trying to— How are you doing?"

I told him about my job. I made it sound more interesting than it really was.

"Are you happy?" He said it soberly, like a therapist.

"Sure, I'm having a blast." I looked out the window behind me at a gridlock of taxicabs on the street below.

"You sound funny. Are you sure you're okay?"

After he said it, I did feel funny—as if somebody were watching me—and turned in my chair to see Greta standing in the doorway of my office.

I had no idea how long she'd been there.

I pointed at the receiver and mouthed the word, "My father."

I expected her to go away, but instead she shuffled in and took a seat across from my desk. She picked up a newspaper and began rifling through it noisily.

My father's voice: "Have you at least made new friends?"

I cleared my throat. "Actually, one of my friends just walked in. Greta. Greta Hicks. She works with me."

Greta perked up at the mention of her name.

"Greta? What is she? A Swede?" To my father, everybody was a social science experiment. He wanted to know where each person he encountered fit into the historical paradigm.

"Half German and half black."

"German and black? How'd that happen?"

"Well, her dad was a GI in World War Two."

Greta nodded, and whispered to me, "Tell him my father liberated the Jews!"

"Her father," I said, slightly annoyed, "liberated the Jews. That's where he met her mother."

"Liberated the Jews? How old is she?"

"Forty. She's in her forties."

"Forty-three," she corrected.

"Forty-three."

"What about friends your age?"

I wanted to tell him about Andrew—how I'd sort of gotten off to a bad start in the ciy, how I hadn't really found a world that felt right in this cold new place. But he'd only say, "I told you so," and besides, Greta was watching me.

"What's he saying about me?"

I jabbered into the phone. "Anyway, she's great. You'd really love her. Interesting. Smart. Funny—"

"And tell him how I found you a place to live."

"She found me a place—"

Just then a recorded Arabic voice cut into the phone line. My father shouted over it that his calling card was running out of money. He was about to be disconnected. "Love you, baby! I'll be in touch soon. *Inshallah*."

AT HOULIHAN'S THAT NIGHT, Greta asked me questions about my family. She wanted to know if I got along with them.

"I do and I don't. I always wished they were different, growing up. More like the families on television. I used to say to them, 'Why can't we be a real family?' And they'd all laugh—my brother included—because I was the only one who didn't think we were real. They were having a grand old time. But to me—well, they always seemed made-up. Like a great idea that only works on paper. Pretty crazy, huh?"

"Not at all. They sound insane."

I bristled. I was allowed to talk badly about them, but nobody else was. "No they're not. They're really not. They're just a little—out of it. You know, they believe children should be given complete freedom. And sometimes I wished they'd given me a little more, well, structure. It's like, they were the kind of parents who don't give you a reason to leave home. And everybody has to leave home, you know?"

"Of course you do! And from the sounds of it, they wouldn't notice you were gone. I mean, you could be dead for all they know."

"Well, I'm not dead. And I wish you wouldn't worry so much."

"I know, I know. Of course you're not dead. You're a big girl, brimming with life and possibility, the golden love child of those wonderfully zany sixties parents who still speak to each other! It's a story of inspiration!"

She was bellowing, her eyes fixed on a spot over my shoulder as if she were addressing somebody behind me.

Now she lowered her gaze on me and said quietly, "But that's not the whole story, is it? That's just the propaganda they made you swallow, like a spoonful of castor oil every day, because it made them feel noble. But the truth is, they don't give a hoot what happens to you. They only care about themselves."

I stared into my drink. A malaise slid through me, then was gone.

When I looked up, she was smiling at me through shining eyes. "You know what? Fuck 'em: your parents and mine, both. They can fall off the edge of the earth for all I care. Because we've got each other. Right?"

I looked at her in silence. Bilious. That was the word. Greta was a bilious woman. I'd seen glimmers of it before, but not like this. She was coming into focus, like Andrew had that night. I remembered something Lola had said to me. We were lying on our backs in the foothills, watching the sky and making a list called "Never." All the things we would never do. *Let's never get married. Let's never get fat. Let's never sleep with a married man. Let's never stop being students, even after we graduate. Let's never get dull-eyed and ironic. Let's never get stuck in a rut—or trapped in a life we didn't choose. Let's never grow bitter.*

There was dandruff on Greta's shoulders. Lots of it. For some reason it disgusted me, and I had to look away. An idea crossed my mind: Tomorrow I would call Lola's parents in Montclair, New Jersey, and find out her latest contact info in Africa. I would call her long-distance from work and talk to her on the company dime. Surely she was coming home soon. Maybe she would stop in New York on her way to the West Coast and stay a few days, with me, in Vera's apartment. It was hard to picture her there. It didn't matter. We wouldn't spend much time in the apartment. We'd do what real New Yorkers do, and eat out every night, and afterward we'd go to the East Village and hang out in bars with people our age. The thought cheered me and I managed a smile at Greta. She smiled back.

13

I CALLED LOLA'S HOME the next afternoon. Her father answered the phone. He was friendly enough, but told me Lola was unreachable, en route to South Africa to stay with friends in Durban. He wouldn't know her contact information for another week. He asked me questions about myself. How was the new job? How was life in the real world? But I could hear a sports game on in the background and suspected he was just being polite. I asked him to tell Lola to write or call me, and he promised he would, but he sounded distracted, and I wasn't sure he really would.

Later that day I got good news: Rula Maven assigned me a real story—not the usual blather I'd been writing, but a profile of an artist. He was, she said, "young, hip, totally inscrutable," and she wanted me to interview him for the arts section. His name was Ivers Greene. She handed me the file and then breezed off down the hall, telling me to get her something by next Tuesday.

I flipped through the file, looking for something tangible—a photo of the artist, or biographical details about him—but I found only glossy reproductions of his work. They were snapshots, photographs of utterly unremarkable people doing utterly unremarkable things. People waiting in line at a bank. People talking on cellular phones in their cars in traffic. People eating at McDonald's. People on the subway.

I stared at the pictures and looked for patterns, auras, referents, the way I'd learned to do in my college art history survey. And, after a while, what struck me was that the people in the pictures had been caught in the most unattractive angles possible. They appeared ghoulish. A businessman eating a piece of McDonald's apple pie had been transformed by the camera angle into a piglet, his nostrils turned up as he shoved the food into his mouth. A woman talking on her cell phone was laughing, and while she may have been attractive in real life, in the split second that the shutter had snapped, she appeared as wrinkled and hunched and contorted as a witch. The photos were the duds that would have been discarded by another photographer, the ones that would have never been allowed in the family album. This artist had not only salvaged these images, but he'd blown them up, put them in a fancy gallery, and transformed them into art.

And then there was the doodle. He'd scribbled into the corner of each photo with a Magic Marker. It was a creature—what appeared to be half monkey, half poodle. It had the long arms and potbelly of an orangutan, with the pointed nose and curly pom-pom ears and Afro puffs of a well-groomed poodle. The creature was an observer at the edge of each photo—grinning wickedly at the subject. In some, it was well hidden. In the bank photograph, I had to search to find it perched on the shoulder of one of the distant tellers. In others, it was literally just a shadow, its profile like a finger puppet against a lit wall.

"Howdy doody," a voice said.

It was Greta standing in the door. I felt a prickle of irritation at the sight of her.

"Houlihan's?"

I shook my head, relieved, for once, to have an excuse. "Can't. Not tonight. I'm wiped out. Besides, I've got this assignment."

She came inside and looked at my desk. "Whatcha lookin' at?"

She picked up a journal. It was open to a reproduction of Greene's photographs. "They call this shit art? I could have done this myself with my disposable Fuji."

"I think that might be the point." I stood and began to gather my things together to go home.

"Whatever," she said, holding a picture out in front of her. "This guy's got a good thing going. We're in the wrong racket, baby. So what's he look like?" She was still flipping through the journal. "Ivers? What kinda name is that?"

"Beats me."

"I'm gonna guess he looks like Elton John: squat faggot with a toupee." She tossed the journal at me. "You like Elton John?"

I shrugged. "He's all right."

"I love him," she said matter-of-factly.

We started out of the office together.

"And anybody who says they don't like him is a liar."

She grabbed my arm as we stepped into the empty elevator, and began to sing aloud, *"My gift is my song, and this one's for you."*

She sang to me, off-tune, the whole ride down, and when the doors opened into the lobby, Ward Anderson—the silver-haired publisher of the magazine—stood on the other side holding a cup of coffee. He frowned at us and I was about to say hello, but Greta pulled me past him, spitting laughter into her hand all the way through the revolving doors.

"I wish you wouldn't do that," I said when we were outside. She'd been rude, and I had looked rude by association. My cheeks were burning. "I wanted to at least say a proper hello."

She rolled her eyes. I hadn't noticed it before, but her affect—the way she moved and huffed and even giggled sometimes—was like an adolescent, not a woman her age. Now she crossed her arms, sulkily, and looked away toward traffic. "Oh please," she said. "They're not gonna rescind your scholarship just 'cause you didn't say a 'proper hello,' as you put it. But you're right. Next time let's stop and curtsey to our benefactor."

"That wasn't my point." I wondered for the first time if it was bad for my reputation at work to be seen around so much with Greta. Did that sort of thing—whom you ate your lunch with, whom you stepped off the elevator with—matter?

She turned to face me, and I was surprised at how distressed she looked. "Forgive me? Please?"

I didn't want to continue the conversation. "Of course. It's no big deal."

She grabbed my hand. "I would never do anything, intentionally, to jeopardize your fellowship. I'm really sorry." She chewed her lip as she watched my face.

I pulled my hand away and stuck it in my pocket. "Don't mind me. I'm just PMSing. Really. I get like this the week before."

"Just like me!"

She was smiling wide now, but her eyes had stayed serious, anxious, as they searched my face for signs that we were okay.

We started toward the subway station together. She chattered beside me about premenstrual syndrome—remedies I should buy. "No, scratch that. Don't spend a dime. I'll bring them into work for you tomorrow."

I was quiet beside her, imagining my evening alone: A little supper. A glass of wine. Curled up on the sofa, playing old seventies records from Vera's collection, doing prep work on the Ivers Greene article. Maybe a bath before bed. It took me a moment to realize I was eager to get back there, to the solitude and privacy of that sublet. Anywhere could start to feel like home if you slept there enough nights.

14

A FEW DAYS LATER, I went off to meet Ivers Greene. It was late in the afternoon. The sky over Chelsea was blank, white as an untouched canvas. The air was icy and still and hurt my lungs. I'd only spoken to his dealer, a haughty fellow named Georgio who had suggested a coffee shop called Les Deux Gamins. I found the place and paused out front to stare in the window. I didn't know exactly who to look for. An artist? The place was cluttered with men who could have fit the bill, all vaguely asexual, the women hard, thin, chain-smoking thirty-somethings dressed in black.

I remembered what Greta had said. Elton John. I settled on a pale squat man with a mop of brown hair, wearing a black turtleneck and horn-rimmed glasses. He sat smoking, flipping through a newspaper, occasionally glancing up at the door as if he were waiting for somebody. I went inside and started toward his table. But just before I got there, from the back of the café came a bang and clatter. I turned to see the bathroom door fly open. A man stumbled out, cursing. He was not much older than me, dark chocolate skin with tiny exclamation-point dreadlocks poking out of his head. He stared for a beat at the people in the café who had looked up to see what the racket was. "Damn lock," he said, and sauntered over to the table just next to Elton John and slid into a seat. I stood between the two tables, unsure now which was the artist. Only when I glanced down at the black man's table did it become clear. He'd begun to draw a sketch on the napkin beside his coffee cup. It was of his table neighbor. In the sketch, he'd exaggerated the man's simian features so that he looked more ape than human.

I watched him for a moment as he filled in the lines of the drawing with a charcoal pencil, then I cleared my throat. "Ivers Greene?" He glanced up, but his eyes darted quickly away from my face down to the drawing on the table. I extended my hand and told him my name. "I'm the reporter from the magazine."

He shifted around in his seat, twisted a dread, stared down at his work. "Oh, hey, yeah. The article."

I sat down across from him and took off my coat. "I hope you weren't waiting long."

"Naw, just a few minutes."

"Are you hungry?"

"Who picked this place anyway?"

"Your dealer."

He scoffed under his breath. "Fucker. I hate this scene. I hate Chelsea. He knows that." He stood up from the table, nearly knocking over the chair he'd been in, and handed the man next to him the sketch he'd done, saying, simply, "Here." While the man stared at it with flared nostrils, Ivers dug into his jeans pocket and threw a grimy five-dollar bill onto the table to pay for his coffee.

I picked up his five, put down my own, tore off the bottom of the check, careful not to meet the eyes of the man beside me who was still staring at the sketch on the napkin.

Out on the street, Ivers leaned against a lamppost, watching me with bored, petulant eyes.

I handed him his filthy bill. "This is on the magazine."

"Really?"

"Really."

He looked pleased as he shoved the money back in his pocket. "We're rich and free," he said. "Let's go to Harlem."

UPTOWN, Ivers kept changing his mind about where he wanted to go for the interview. I followed two paces behind him as we zigzagged along 125th Street. First he wanted to go to Sylvia's, the world-famous purveyor of soul food. Then, when we were only half a block away, he changed his mind and stood in the middle of the sidewalk, explaining that, no, he didn't want to go there after all. He'd forgotten that he hated that place. Before I could ask why, he pointed at a Jamaican greasy spoon across the street and, without warning, began to jaywalk across the thoroughfare, calling back to me over his shoulder, "C'mon!"

When I reached him on the other side, he was staring in through the steamed glass of Evelyn's Jamaican Jerk. I peered in, too. People sat hunched over tiny tables, eating chicken and roti off styrofoam plates. "Looks good," I said, based on nothing more than the speed with which the people were shoveling the food into their open mouths and the smell of spices that drifted out when somebody opened the door.

But Ivers shook his head. "Yuck," he said, staring wistfully up and down the block. He squinted at something far in the distance. "Of course, Roylstons," and started down the block in the direction we'd come from.

ƧOI | *103*

126TH STREET. Roylstons Bar and Lounge. The place was sprinkled with customers—men with bulbous noses and bloodshot eyes. Gerald LeVert was playing, and a couple grooved on the dance floor slowly, pressed against each other. The man's hand kept moving down over the woman's ample behind. Each time she would laugh, with her head thrown back, and push his mitts back up to her waist.

Ivers and I sat at the bar, sipping white wine with ice cubes floating in the glasses and picking at a bowl of stale popcorn.

"Tell me about the poodle-monkey."

"Poodle-monkey?"

"The creature. The one in all your photographs."

"Oh, you must mean Menchu."

"Okay, Menchu."

"He's not a poodle-monkey, though I could see why you might think that. He's—well, let's just say he doesn't like labels."

"Um, okay. What does he represent to you? Why is he in all the pictures?"

Ivers looked at me, perfectly serious. "He isn't in *all* the pictures. He's only in some of them. In others, you can only see his shadow. The thing is this: Sometimes when I brought him along for the shoot he'd get all weird and shy, refuse to get in the picture. So I'd have to shoot his shadow. That's Menchu for you."

"You talk about Menchu as if he's real," I said in my reporter's voice.

Ivers stared back at me, dull-eyed, not cracking the slightest smile. The waitress came to give us refills. She was a pretty, plum brown girl with elaborate ribbons of multi-colored hair piled on top of her head. She cut her eyes at me and addressed only Ivers when she took our orders.

When she was gone, I forged on with the interview. "Okay. Let's see. Do you agree with the writer Joel Zedman, who wrote of your last show, 'Ivers Greene shows us humanity in its most ghoulish light. . . . His paintings are a clarion warning to us at the end of the century.' And if you do agree with him, I guess I'm wondering what are you warning us about?"

Ivers didn't appear to be listening. He was frowning at my face so intently that I thought there was something on it. I wiped at my cheek, then the other, rubbed my nose, but there was nothing there.

"Can I ask you a question?"

"Yeah."

He whispered it. "Are you a quadroon?"

I turned away quickly so he wouldn't see the surprise on my face. I took a gulp of my wine. "No," I said. "That's not the word I'd use to describe myself." I looked back at him. "I'm half. And anyway, that word just seems pretty archaic."

His mouth curled into a slight smile. "Oh. You don't like that kind of language. It's impolite. You must be one of those 'new people' I keep reading about in the papers."

"I guess so," I said.

He began to laugh then. It was a tinkle at first. But it grew into a full belly laugh.

"What's so funny?"

He sighed happily at the joke he refused to share. "Lemme ask you another question."

I waved the reporter's notebook at him. "Later. See, I've got a lot more questions for *you*—"

"But—well—I'm so curious. I've just got to know."

"Okay. What?"

He leaned in, and once again spoke in a whisper. "Do you say 'motherfucker'?" He said the word all stiff and nasal. "Or do you say 'muthafucka'?" This time he said this word in a high, exaggerated slang.

I fixed my gaze on the ice cubes floating in the wineglass.

Ivers repeated the question. "Do you say 'motherfucker,' or do you say 'muthafucka'? 'Cause you could really go either way with somebody like you."

I took a sip of my drink.

"I asked you a question," he persisted. "Do you say 'motherfucker'? Or 'muthafucka'? Which one?"

I stood up and grabbed my coat and bag, threw a twenty on the counter.

"Hey," he said. "Where are you going?"

"Fuck you," I said. "I say, 'Fuck you,' " and stormed out of Roylstons.

It was night. Dirty cars like tin cans moved past slowly in traffic, a stream of exhaust and beeping. The sky was invisible, a clutter of billboards for liquor and cigarettes and cars and insurance. Lots of insurance. Empty-eyed models grinned ecstatically down at the pedestrians trudging home slowly as if their bunions were aching.

I headed around a corner, into an alley, where I paused to put on my coat. When I had it on I peeked back around in the direction I'd come from.

Sure enough, Ivers had followed me outside. He stood there, in the middle of the block in front of Roylstons, no coat on, looking plaintively to his left and right.

After a while, he turned and made his way back inside.

Only then did I emerge from my hiding place and jog toward the subway station a few blocks away.

ON THE TRAIN headed downtown, I stood squeezed in between a decrepit old man and a pregnant young woman clutching a metal pole. Nobody had offered them a seat. Instead, the seats were filled with the young and able, who sat with their legs sticking out where somebody could trip over them.

As I stood there, I found myself thinking not about what had just occurred but about something from my past—somebody I'd dated in college. Claude. In general I tried not to think about him. My only recourse had been to ban him from my memory. But sometimes, like now, he drifted back into my thoughts whether I liked it or not.

We'd met during the fall of my junior year. He was a teaching assistant in my class "Images of Blacks in Film." It was a popular course, and I'd taken it because it was known to be easy. There was only one book you had to read, called *Toms, Coons, Mammies, Mulattos, and Bucks*. The professor was a kindly old man who wanted to retire and until that day would only teach courses where he could sit in the dark and watch movies.

Claude was ten years older than me. Dreadlocks. Pale yellow skin. Angular features. A Ph.D. student in African American studies. He and a smattering of other teaching assistants did all the grading and met with us one-on-one throughout the semester.

One day he invited me to coffee to discuss topics for my final paper. I'd never talked to him alone before. We sat in a booth at the back of the Coffee House, "Sweet Home Alabama" blaring over the speakers. He told me that I had beautiful hands and feet, long, delicate "whispers of Africa," as he put it.

Later that semester, lying beside me on the futon bed in his graduate student housing suite, he preferred to call them my "permanent reminders." Just like the rest of my body. He said it was a "permanent reminder" of what I still held within me.

One night, when things were beginning to erode between me and Claude, he predicted my future. It was late. We were in a bar off campus. He had just put back three pints of Guinness draft on an empty stomach.

"Oh, I see it all," he'd said. "You'll end up on a farm someday in Vermont, with a husband named Ben and a kid named Chloe or Zoë or Max. And you'll remember all this as just a phase you were going through. And when the day comes when your marriage starts to go a little stale, because they all do, you will tell your husband about your dark past. You'll tell him about the black boys you loved or didn't love and the protests you attended or didn't attend, and when you're done talking he will fuck you in the dark, and the sex will have never been better. And you will be thankful for this past. And thankful that it is over."

Six months later we had sex for the last time in my dorm room. It was midafternoon. My mind wasn't really on his touches, and my eyes kept drifting out the window to the palm trees. They looked to me like a row of lean brown boys with dreadlocks sprouting out from their heads. The sky over them was a dusky orange. Down Lomita Drive, I could see a cluster of students walking in and out of the Student Health Center.

When it was over, I lay with my back to him, feeling his

cold sticky residue seep out onto my thighs and the camel-colored sheets, and listening as he told me it was over.

"Don't take it personally," he said, stroking my back with his fingers. "It's just that, well, I don't feel at home with you. At the end of the day, I don't feel comforted when I see your face. And when you get to my age, that's what you're looking for. Comfort."

For some reason I couldn't concentrate on what he was saying. The television was on, though the sound was off. The show that played was an old episode of *Three's Company.* Mr. Roper was at the door, holding a plunger and a bucket. Jack was trying to get rid of him. Inside the apartment, behind the front door, you could see that Jack was hiding a half-dressed blonde.

"It's like, I know you've got it in you, somewhere, 'cause I've seen your family photo. And," Claude said with a chuckle, "I've seen this." He patted my derriere. "But when I look at your face, I see something else. And it's unsettling. You know? The dissonance."

Mr. Roper was inside the apartment now, whistling as he sauntered past the half-dressed blonde, oblivious to her quivering form. As soon as Mr. Roper was in the bathroom, Jack hustled the bimbo out the door, but at the same moment, Mrs. Roper, in a muumuu, walked in the door. Hand on hip, she eyed the woman. I could read her lips. *What is this we have here?*

"Are you even listening to me?"

His dreadlocks were tickling my arm like a tentacle reaching out to me.

"Yeah, you're leaving me. I've fallen short."

I rolled over to look at him—but at the sight of his face I lost control. I buried my face in the pillow and began to laugh. It was the kind of laughter that always overtook me at funerals—overwhelming and completely bewildering to me and everyone around me. My face was hidden, and Claude assumed I was crying and patted my shoulder, clucking his teeth. "I'm sorry. I didn't mean to hurt you. We can still be friends."

He kissed my shoulder, and pulled me over to face him.

He saw that I was laughing. First he looked stricken, then angry. "What the fuck?"

I wiped my tears with the back of my hand. "I'm sorry, I can't help it."

He pulled his hand away from my shoulder as if I were contagious. He tried to laugh, too, to regain some control of the situation maybe. But the laughter died as soon as it had risen to his lips, and he muttered, "Guess it's true what they say."

That was the last thing he said to me. *Guess it's true what they say.*

I didn't know what he meant, and I didn't bother asking. I just watched, holding my stomach, still laughing, as he got up and walked naked across my room, past the sliding glass doors, his bare bottom and dangling penis exposed to the whole campus. He dressed quickly, threw me a final angry look, picked up his shoulder bag and the book he'd be teaching a gaggle of undergraduates that afternoon—*Mules and Men*—and walked out my door forever.

Only after he was gone did it stop being funny. And I spent the rest of the afternoon lying in bed watching situation comedy after situation comedy in sober silence.

SYMPTOMATIC

SOMEBODY WAS WATCHING ME. I was sure of it. I looked up into the faces on the subway car around me. A white girl. The only one here tonight. I stared back at her, irritated by the expression on her face, a slight, searching smile, as if she thought we were comrades among all these dark bodies. That happened to me a lot. The one white person on board smiled at me as if to say, *Thank God you're here. We can help each other in case there is a riot.*

This girl was neither beautiful nor ugly, but she stood out on that subway car like a firefly in the country night. She had medium-length brown hair, a pointy face. Fullish lips for a white girl. Brown eyes. She was dressed kind of like me: a tan corduroy jacket that wasn't warm enough for the weather, an Irish fisherman's sweater underneath, and black slacks. And she was staring at me. I was sure of it. Staring at me and copying everything I did. When I blinked, she blinked. When I scratched my head, she scratched her head. Now she was even aping my own slumped posture and bereft expression. I felt an irrational rage well up inside of me—an urge to go over and slap her until she stopped looking at me. *What? What? You see something funny?* I restrained myself. I rode with her mimicking me the whole way. She didn't get off the subway until my stop in Brooklyn. She started toward the door at the same moment that I did, glancing over at me nervously as if to make sure I was still there. I wanted to follow her—to ask what it was she saw that made her gape—but as soon as we were off the train, she vanished.

GRETA CALLED ME THAT NIGHT as I was drifting off to sleep.

"Uh-oh," she said when she heard my voice. "Did I wake you up?"

She was at a pay phone. I could hear cars whooshing past behind her.

"No," I lied, propping myself up on an elbow. "I was still awake. What's up?"

She took a sharp inhalation from a cigarette, then said, "Just wanted to know how the interview went. You know. With Elton."

The clock across the room read twelve-thirty. I rubbed my eyes. "Terrible," I said. "As bad as an interview could possibly go." Then I told her what had happened, what he'd said to me. *Motherfucker or muthafucka.* "Over and over again. He just wouldn't stop. So I told him to fuck off and walked out."

I waited for her laugh, because it sounded almost funny, but she was angry. "Typical prick," she said. "God! You did the right thing. Assholes like that, they're out for only one thing: to humiliate us. Mark my words. He should be taken out and shot—"

"It's okay," I said quickly. "I mean, I'm fine. Anyway, I've got to worry about what to tell Rula tomorrow. The article's a wash. She's gonna have my scalp."

"Oh, don't worry," Greta said. "I'll figure something out. Just give me a night to sleep on it."

"What do you mean?"

I heard a wild screeching and a crash in the background,

somewhere behind Greta, then a man shouting, "What are you, blind?"

"Jesus, what an asshole," Greta said, momentarily distracted. "Anyway, now go back to sleep. Don't worry about a thing. I'm gonna go put on my thinking cap, and in the morning, we'll sort this whole thing out. Night-night."

AFTERWARD, I couldn't get comfortable. First I was too cold, then too hot. Shivering, I pulled the comforter over me, then, a few minutes later, sweaty and breathless, I pushed it off onto the floor. I felt a bug crawling up my leg. But when I searched for it, I found nothing. The sheets smelled like somebody else's skin. And when I shut my eyes, I heard noises everywhere: a faucet dripping, a distant car alarm, the ticking of my own watch. It was almost morning when I finally fell into a tangled, uneasy sleep.

15

ELL RULA he tried to rape you," Greta said. "Tell her he pinned you to a table and you had to fight like hell to escape unviolated. That should appeal to her feminist sensibilities."

We were sitting across from each other in a dingy Chinese food restaurant near the office.

I laughed, lightly, nervously, but she didn't crack a smile.

"Come on, that's insane. I'm not going to say that."

"Why not? It'd get you off the hook. She wouldn't dare send you back into his clutches."

"I think I'll just tell her the truth."

Greta scoffed. "Right. Like that cracker bitch is gonna understand anything." She sighed heavily and pushed her tray away. "But suit yourself."

She was in a bad mood. I had not yet seen her in such a mood.

I watched her face as she stared at the people moving along 53rd Street. She looked like she was coming down with something. Dark circles under her eyes. Cracked lips. Today she was wearing the wrong color—a sweater in mustard yellow. It made her look sick.

"Hey," I said. "Are you feeling okay? You seem—"

She looked back at me. "I hate to be the one to break the news to you, kid, but life sucks. You'll learn. Someday. You think it's all hunky-dory." She made her voice high to imitate me. "That you can get out of a muddle by telling the truth." She shook her head. "But it doesn't work that way."

"I do appreciate your advice."

Singsong repetition. "'I do appreciate your advice.'" She pressed her fingers to her temple and closed her eyes. "I'm sorry. Don't mind me. It just gets hard sometimes. You try to keep going, but for what?"

"You've got a lot going for you," I said, but the words sounded weak.

"Yeah," Greta said, with a slight twist of a smile. "A dead-end job. A crappy roach-infested apartment, a whole freezer full of Lean Cuisines. Mmmmm good."

"That makes two of us," I said, trying to lighten the conversation. "I'm so sick of Ho Ho's takeout I could puke."

"Two of us? Honey, you're the *Riggs Fellow.* And you're, like, thirteen years old. We are not in the same boat. Trust me."

I coughed, then said, "You're a beautiful intelligent woman." Like a sentence you'd learn in a Berlitz course. When she didn't reply, just scowled, I said, "Maybe you should try to meet somebody. As in, start dating."

She made a sound in her throat—it wasn't quite a laugh—and turned to look at me. "Date?" she said, as if the word were Mandarin. "Who would I date?"

Her lips curled into a small, sardonic smile. "Middle-aged cow with bunions on her toes and a bad case of secretarial spread. In search of—" She picked up her napkin and draped it over her food like a sheet across a corpse. "You fill in the rest, kid, 'cause I've tried every variation in the book and let me tell you, girls like us, we don't mix well. The black guys just want to put us down, drag us through the dirt, work out their fucking insecurity complexes on us. And the white ones. Well, sister, I don't have to tell you about the white ones, do I?"

I noticed as she spoke that her eyes fixed just slightly—almost imperceptibly—to the left of my face. It gave me the odd sensation that there was somebody hovering behind me. I wondered if it was an optical defect, something I'd never noticed before. I moved my face slightly to enter her line of vision, but she moved her eyes, too, as if following this shadow person, not me.

"Well," I said. "What about a mixed guy? Have you ever tried that?"

"A mixed guy? That would be a bit redundant, don't you think?"

I didn't answer. She was looking away, toward the waiter, the corners of her mouth turned down like a comic-book frown. I watched her profile, wondering if bitterness could be contagious.

We left the restaurant in silence. It was snowing—big flakes drifting like pale ashes from a distant fire.

As we made our way back to the office, Greta's mood seemed to lift slightly. She chattered about a facialist named Helga she wanted to take me to. Helga was an expert at skin like ours, she said, the sole reason Greta looked so much younger than she was. Helga would do beautiful things to my eyebrows.

About a block from the office, I stopped in my tracks. For a moment, I thought I was mistaken—an optical illusion created by a trick of light. I squinted through the snow. It was no mistake. It was him. Ivers Greene. Standing in front of our office building, playing with a yo-yo.

Greta turned around to see why I'd stopped.

"That's him, the artist. The one I was telling you about."

"That skinny black guy?"

The sight of him standing there made me laugh into my mitten. "Oh my God. How funny is that?"

Greta put a hand on her hip. "I don't think it's funny at all. I think it's creepy. You aren't actually going to speak to him after yesterday, are you?"

"I'll see what he wants."

We started to walk. Greta spoke with her face tilted down, eyes peeking up at Ivers in the distance. "I'll tell you what he wants. He wants to get in your underpants."

He stood slouched against the building, one foot resting against the wall behind him. The yo-yo was one of those glow-in-the-dark ones from a dime store. He was giving it his full concentration, brow furrowed, biting his bottom lip, but he was doing a lousy job. Every time it went down, it stayed down, and he had to wind it up again manually.

Greta was still talking. "Listen, I think you should think twice about going back there. A guy like that only wants—"

I turned to her. "Hey, don't worry about me, okay? I'm just gonna have a few words with him, maybe finish this interview after all." I tried to joke. "Maybe he's ready for his close-up."

But she didn't laugh. Her face was drawn with fear, and I felt sorry for her. I shouldn't have confided in her. She was making way too big a deal out of this—out of everything—but I didn't know how to explain that to her.

She glanced over at him. "He looks like an inmate, with that crazy pickaninny hair—"

I put a hand on her shoulder. "It's okay. Please. Just go upstairs. Let me handle this."

She threw me one final disapproving look as she went inside.

IVERS WAS SO FOCUSED on the yo-yo he didn't seem to see me.

"Hey," I said, when I was directly in front of him.

He didn't look up at me. Just said, "You know how to get these knickknacks to work?"

The yo-yo hung limply at the end of its string. Ivers groaned and began to wind it up. When he was done he put it in his pocket and only then did he glance up at me. We both kind of laughed when our eyes met, as if the other had told a mildly funny joke.

"What are you doing here?"

"I'm freezing my butt off. That's what." He struggled to look serious. "Listen. About yesterday. I was just trying to make you laugh. But I pissed you off instead. Or something. Sorry. I'm not good at interviews. Can we try again?"

I hesitated, then glanced over my shoulder. "There's a café across the street. I'm not going back to Roylstons."

"Yeah, yeah, yeah," he grumbled. "This'll be just fine."

We started down the block the way I'd come. As we passed the office lobby, I glanced inside. Greta stood huddled behind the glass, watching us, her arms folded, her eyes great black pits of worry. I waved my hand—part greeting, part dismissal—but she didn't move or blink. She just continued staring at us, wide-eyed, as if she were witnessing extra-terrestrial life strolling down Madison Avenue.

THIS TIME Ivers answered my questions. All of them. He sat stiffly across from me in the crowded French café with his hands folded on the table, talking loudly and precisely into my tape recorder's microphone. I told him he could relax and sit back, the tape would pick him up. But he didn't seem to believe me and remained hunched over the small black box ar-tic-u-lat-ing very slowly and clearly as he answered each question. He told me who his influences were (the late, great Houdini and the filmmaker Roman Polanski), what he was working on now (a project involving stolen hospital goods), and where he'd thought up the creature Menchu (it was named after the Guatemalan peasant and memoirist Rigoberta Menchú).

When I asked him about his childhood, where he was from, he leaned away from the tape recorder. "I grew up under a rock. An earthworm."

I nodded. "Great. I'll be sure to mention that."

As I started to put my tape recorder and notebook away, he said, "Hey, you know who you remind me of?"

I stiffened. "No. Who?"

"Kristy McNichol."

"As in the actress?"

"Yeah. From *Little Darlings*. I don't know why. It's just—I don't know. Something about you. Real seventies. Like, your hair isn't feathered, but it should be."

"Well, thanks, I guess."

I reached across the table for my pen, and he pointed at my arm. "Plus, you got hairy arms."

I glanced at my arm. I'd rolled up my sweater sleeve, and my forearm was exposed. He was right: I'd always had hairy arms. I'd always been ashamed of them. Tried different methods of removal, including bleaching. But since I'd left Andrew, I'd let myself go. Nobody to witness my body. Nobody to praise my efforts, so why bother. And so here the hair sat, weeds in an untended garden: dark hairs that lay against my pale skin.

I pulled my arm away and quickly rolled down my sleeve, cheeks burning.

"It was a compliment. Hairy arms are nice."

Outside on the sidewalk we stood awkwardly facing one another, but both reading the pavement. The snow was sticking. I glanced across the street trying to think of what to say next.

A person dressed in a purple ski cap and a beige trench coat darted behind a parked van, hunched down low behind the passenger-side window, watching us through the glass.

"What's the matter?"

I looked back at him.

He frowned, quizzically. "You changed just then. What is it?"

I glanced back at the van.

"Um, nothing." I scratched my head. My words were a desperate rush. "Listen, you want to go out sometime? I mean, just hang out. I only moved to the city, well, pretty recently. Actually, this past summer. But I don't know that many people my age."

I felt stupid after I said it, but also distracted by what was going on across the street.

From behind the van, the person was bobbing his or her head—I couldn't tell if it was a he or a she—trying to get a better look at us.

Ivers smiled slightly. "Um, okay. Sure." He laughed. "Listen, it doesn't matter much to me, but I'm just curious. Is that allowed? You know, the journalist and the subject—"

The person crouched down low now out of sight.

I looked back at him. "So, listen, I'll call you."

He laughed. "You're strange—but yeah, call me."

He backed away from me, waved his hand, then turned and was gone.

I waited a moment to see if the person would come out from behind the van. But nobody emerged. After a moment, I ducked my head and started across the street, telling myself it was nothing. Just another weirdo getting his rocks off.

Upstairs in my office I closed the door, sat in my swivel chair in the dark, put on my headphones, and listened to my interview with Ivers Greene. Whom I'd just asked out on a date. It sounded remote, the recording of our voices, like something that had happened a long time ago. And listening to it, I forgot about the person behind the van. I felt giddy and foolish and a little bewildered. I couldn't see the end of the story.

16

"DONE?"

Greta stood in the hallway, dripping wet. Her hair had frizzed up from the melting snowflakes and hung around her face in wiry curls.

I had just finished my article about Ivers. It was ten o'clock at night.

"I thought you'd never finish."

She was wearing a beige trench coat. She had not been wearing it at lunch.

"What are you still doing here?"

"I was waiting to celebrate."

"Celebrate what?"

"You. You finishing the article." She sniffed. "Took you long enough." She rubbed her nose hard with the flat of her palm. "So you coming? We need to get there before they all go home."

"Who goes home?"

"The horsemen at Central Park. I was thinking we could go for a ride. To celebrate."

"At this hour?"

"Come on, don't be a bore. This is New York City."

I felt something—that bug again—crawling along the back of my neck, but I didn't move to swat it away this time.

"No," I started to say, but something on her face made me think better of it. I wanted to keep the peace. Anyway, as far as I knew, the horse-drawn carriages had already gone home—and so if I made the effort of going all the way to the park, I would be off the hook.

"All right," I said. "But just a quick ride."

She didn't break into a grin the way she ordinarily did when I accepted her invitations. She just crinkled her nose and sawed at it harder with her finger, as if she were trying to rub it loose. "Hurry. They're gonna go home soon."

As I'd hoped, we were too late. The horses and the carriages had already been dismantled. An old grizzled man dressed up like a leprechaun in a green pointed hat and vest and shoes that turned up at the toes stood counting money in front of his forlorn beast, as if he were preparing to split the earnings between them.

I hung back while Greta begged him for a ride.

"Come on," she said. "My friend here just finished a big assignment. Can't you take us around once?"

He had an accent thick as a rind. Rolling and rising in soft lilts. "I'm sorry, lass, but I've got to go home. Already packed up. Besides, look at this weather. We'll catch our death out here."

Greta didn't budge. She stood, head bent toward the ground, staring at the old man's leprechaun shoes.

"Please? We'll sit under a blanket. We'll be warm enough. Just take us around once."

"So sorry, m'dear, but I can't do it. Come back a bit earlier tomorrow and I'll gladly take you around. Twice."

"No. Not tomorrow." I heard the escalation in her voice. "Tonight."

I intercepted. "It's okay, Greta. Let's do it tomorrow. We can get a drink. Over there. Look, there's a hotel. I'm sure the bar's open."

She glanced in the direction I pointed at the golden glow of the Ritz-Carlton across the street. She shot the old man a hateful glance. "All right, fine. Thanks a lot, Mickey Rooney."

The old man's face smarted as if he had been slapped, but he didn't say a word.

Her mood seemed to lift once we were inside, seated across from each other in velvet armchairs. She puffed on a Benson & Hedges Menthol, eyeing me through the haze.

When the drinks came, she held up her kamikaze and said, "To Ivers Greene—major asshole that he is. And to the loveliest, brightest Riggs Fellow ever. A rising star in our midst."

I lifted my glass weakly.

The drink itself was the only thing that felt good at that moment.

"What did you write about the great ghetto *artiste* anyway?"

I ignored the sarcasm and tried to sound normal again as I described my article—how I'd opened it, how I'd described Ivers, how I'd closed it.

She nodded as I spoke, a crooked smirk on her face.

When I was finished, she picked up her drink and took a gulp, placed it in front of her, and stared off, over my head, at the snow falling outside.

I tried to fill the silence. "I hope Rula likes it. I tried to keep to the tone of the magazine, but at the same time—"

She interrupted me. "So you've got a boyfriend now."

"Excuse me?"

"Do you love him?"

I laughed a little. "Greta, I don't know what you're talking about. I wrote an article. It was an assignment. Didn't you hear a word I said?"

Her eyes flickered across my face, but then away again. "Yeah. I heard," she said. "You finally got laid by a horse-hung Negro. Pure, uncut, grade-A nigra meat. How did it feel to be penetrated by ole King Kong himself?"

I bit the ice like a piece of glass. My fingers twitched on my knees. "I don't know what your problem is today, Greta. Ivers is not my boyfriend. That's absurd. He's an artist I was assigned to write about."

Greta snickered. "Well, he might not be your boyfriend now, but he will be. Tomorrow or the next day or the day after that. Mark my words. I can tell. You've got that look. Like you're on the prowl. If it's not him, it'll be somebody else. Not a white boy. You're done with that. It'll be some coon with a hankering for high-yella ass. You'll fall head over heels and next thing I know you'll be doing the jitterbug up in Harlem with Mr. Milky Way, discovering your black heritage astride his dick. And I'll just be some sandpile you used to play in."

At a table nearby, a businessman laughed so hard his face turned purple. At the bar, a guy was sticking his tongue into a woman's ear, flicking it in and out like a snake. His tongue had black spots on it—the shape of countries on a map. Was that a disease I hadn't heard of—geographical tongue?

"It's two-faced bitches like you that give us a bad name."

I looked back at her. She was staring so hard I could actually feel it on my forehead. I stood in a rush and made my way across the polished ivory floor toward the ladies' room.

It was posh, marble, with mirrors on all sides. I went into the first stall and bent over the toilet. I began to retch. I hadn't eaten, so it was an empty, violent gagging that brought up only a thin, bitter mixture of coffee and alcohol. Afterward, I leaned against the door, held my stomach, and began to cry quietly. With a sudden, childish hunger, I missed my family, missed the sounds of my parents' voices and my brother's teasing and even the sound of their laughter, mocking me and all my aspirations. I even missed California, Berserkeley, with its ridiculous, dusty idealism. Outside, I could hear the bathroom door swinging open and closed. Women entering and leaving, with their endlessly full bladders.

After a while I came out of the stall, wiping my cheeks.

And there she was, standing at the sink, washing her hands. She stared at me in the reflection. "Oh," she said when she saw I was crying. "You all right?" Her mood had changed again. She turned to face me, wiping her hands on a paper towel.

"Hey there now," she said, tossing the paper towel on the floor. "I was just kidding out there. You don't know how to take a joke."

And through a blur of wetness I saw her swimming toward me. Felt her arms embrace me, her hair tickling my cheek, and the softness of her bosom pressed against my chest. I heard her whispering in my ear, "You're not alone. I'm here. I'm here now." I could smell the cocoa butter on her skin. I felt her hands massaging the back of my skull, its cranial hardness.

"I didn't mean to upset you. God, that's the last thing I wanted to do, it's just I'm so worried about you. I don't want to see you get hurt. I know these guys. They come across so hip and happening, but they always turn on you. They turn on you and—"

Her voice sounded different, thicker. I managed to pull away to see that her eyes were tear-stained, murky, black stones at the bottom of a dirty river, and the skin around them was smudged with wetness. She laughed. "Look what you've done to me. I'm a faucet."

She bit her lip, looked at the floor, then peeked up at me. She seemed to want to say something, but was trying to decide if she should. Finally, she said, "Hey, have I told you my plans for tomorrow night?"

I shook my head.

She shrugged and rolled her eyes and said with weary resignation, "I've got to go to this friend's house and cook her supper, if you can believe it."

I felt relief rush through me. She had another friend. She had plans.

"That sounds really, really nice," I said, stepping backward and leaning against the sink behind me. Water from the counter seeped into the back of my pants, but I didn't move.

She glanced over my shoulder at the mirror behind me, her expression self-conscious, slightly conceited, the way people's expressions tend to be when they are aware of their own reflection. Mirror-face. "This friend of mine? You'd love her," she said, tilting her head down and batting her eyelashes at herself. It was giving me the strange sensation of being surrounded by her—one version of her in front of me and the other behind. "She's wonderful," she said. "Most of the time. But right now? She's having a hard time. She's sad and she's sick, and that's why I'm going to cook for her. She's, like, so sick she can't even cook for herself." She looked back at me and her mouth curled into a teasing smile. I felt a prickle of discomfort return. She continued, "My friend? She thinks she's all alone. She doesn't realize that somebody out there cares about her so much it's breaking that somebody's heart. She doesn't know what a special person she is." She was grinning with her mouth, but her eyes stayed hollow and scared.

I scratched my head. Swallowed. Listened to the sounds—pedestrian, familiar—of the ladies' room. The tinkle of somebody peeing nearby. A cough. An unraveling of toilet paper. The flushing.

Greta raised her eyebrows. "So. Have you guessed who my friend is?"

I didn't say anything, just stared at her.

She whispered, as if to a small child, "It's you. The special girl I have plans to cook for tomorrow night." She reached out and tapped my shoulder with her finger. "You."

I shook my head. "Actually, I'm busy, I have plans to go out—"

She shook her head. "No. No you don't. Not in your condition." She said it like a doctor. "Now why don't you just relax and stay home for once and let somebody take—"

I cut her off. "I'm not in any condition. I'm fine. Really. I'm sorry I broke down."

She smiled and pursed her lips in affectionate disapproval. "Know what? I'm gonna call you Rocky from now on. 'Cause you're tough. Rocky Balboa. Yeah." She put her hands on her hips and puffed out her chest and furrowed her brow and said in a deep voice, "I'm fine. I'm sorry I broke down." She relaxed her affect and shook her head. "You don't have to pretend with me. It's okay to lean on somebody once in a while."

I heard a violent blast of diarrhea from behind one of the stall doors, and an awful smell wafted over to us.

"I've got to get going. I'll be okay. Really." With that, I turned on my heel and started out of the restroom.

She followed, quiet now. She didn't say another word—just picked up her coat when I picked up mine, put on hers when I put on mine, and followed me down the escalator and outside, to the street, where I stood at the curb waiting for a vacant taxi. I held my arm raised high and straight so that a cab would be sure to see me—and when I glanced beside me I saw she was imitating me. She was raising her arm high and straight just like mine, and her face was screwed up in a fierce frown.

She caught my eye and cracked up laughing. "I'm only fooling," she said. "You just look funny."

I turned away. It was freezing, but my cheeks were burning. I saw a cab with its light on and waved at it. In my peripheral vision I could see her still imitating me.

Before the cab had come to a full stop, my hand was on the door. I glanced behind me before getting inside. She was standing there now on the curb, hands returned to her pockets. She looked frumpy and nondescript, and for a moment I wondered if I was overreacting.

"Well," I said, "good night."

"Was it?" she asked, eyes sparkling with meaning.

I got in and slammed the door, and the cab began to move forward, but at the corner there was a red light, and so we idled. I twisted around in my seat and breathed in sharply. There she was, following the car. Jogging after us, with her arm held out in front of her like a cartoon character who has missed a train. She was only a few feet behind us. When she saw my face peering back at her she began to wave and mouth something. I couldn't make out what she was saying, but her lips moved. Something about "I forgot" and "rent"? Or was it "bent"? Before she could reach my window, the light changed, and the cab was moving forward and away. I didn't tell the driver to stop, and I didn't look back again. I just slid down low in the vinyl seat and watched the chaos of colors and motion outside my window.

17

I GOT LOST ONCE, I was just a kid, maybe ten. Somehow, I got separated from my family. We were in Los Angeles for a weekend, visiting my parents' friends—Mohammed, known as Mo, and his wife, Rebecca. Fellow professors. Fellow interracial marriage, an Arab and a Jew. And their three obnoxious kids.

We all went out to lunch in Santa Monica and then walked around afterward, looking in shops. It was hot—as hot as I'd ever felt. The street wobbled before us in the Southern California glare, and Mo's linen shirt was sodden with sweat.

When and where and how I was separated from the group I do not know. In my memory I blame it on the Southern California sun, which I imagine bounced off every surface and blinded me. All I know for certain is that when I looked up to find them, they were all gone. My father, my mother, my brother—and the other family, too.

In those next three hours the streets became a maze of incomprehensible Spanish words, every mini-mall looking alike, and every sunburned face turned mocking and ghoulish, exploding with prosperity. The only other pedestrians were Mexican day workers from Tijuana who spoke no English, and a few drug-crazed white beach bums whom I knew better than to approach. Everybody else slid past in vehicles, a blur of humanity distanced by chrome and glass. I did not ask for help but instead—out of that bizarre pride that overcomes some of us when we are at our most desperate—made a show of pretending I was actually not lost at all. I was careful not to walk past the same café too many times, leaned against a random car in a parking lot as if I were waiting for my mother to come out with groceries any minute, wandered through shops pretending I was going to buy something, and sat on the lawn down near the water watching a juggler amuse a crowd of happy strangers. At one point I even pretended to talk on a pay phone simply to avoid one particularly concerned-looking woman with a baby who had seen me circling the parking lot and must have caught the panicked look on my face. I mouthed words and feigned a casual laugh at the dial tone on the other end.

I don't know how long I wandered, but at some point I could wander no more. I sat down on a bus stop bench. It was getting late. The sky had turned a bleary commuter orange. The traffic was getting thicker. Cars moved slow as slugs onto the freeway, away from the sea. I curled over onto my knees and hid my face behind my hands and did not move from this position for a long time. Buses came and went from the stop and the air grew cool around me, and from behind my palms I sensed it was night.

And when I heard a man's voice saying my name, I thought I was imagining things—but I moved my hands away. Sure enough, a police car sat idling at the curb in front of me.

I could see my parents in the backseat. And my brother's dirty-blond Afro between them. They were all smiling. Even the policeman. Their white teeth shone in the darkness of the vehicle. I thought they were all laughing at me, amused by the sight of me, dirty and bereft at a bus station.

I did not move. I just sat there staring at them as if I were waiting not for them but for a bus back to Tijuana where my real family lived. I sat there staring until the policeman released the safety lock on the back door and my father was able to get out and pick me up in his arms.

That night Mo and Rebecca cooked a celebratory meal of falafel and baba ghanoush, and my brother and the other kids played a raucous game of Pictionary in the living room. I sat fidgeting by the window, staring out at the freeway in the distance. That stream of lights and the deserted city streets described the world for me now, and not here, this bright full space of laughter and friends.

This is the strange effect of getting lost. You become aware not so much of what is absent—all that is familiar and safe—but rather of what that familiarity has been keeping at bay: a world of strange shadows and cruel laughter, of odious companions just waiting for you to come out and play. And they know you will.

18

I SPENT ALL DAY hiding in my office, the door shut, editing my story. Rula liked the Ivers Greene article; he was, she said, a "real basket case," but fascinating, and I'd done a graceful job of describing his work and influences. She only wished I'd included more about where he came from. It would run next week with my byline. And she had another story idea for me to work on. A New Age cult. She wanted me to research the organization and get back to her next week with what I thought was the best angle. She handed me a file of clippings, and I thanked her for the opportunity.

I slipped out of work early and wandered the city aimlessly for the next three hours, finding comfort in being no place at all. I walked through the Village trying on clothes, flipping through used records and books, none of which I bought. I sat in a café reading a magazine and sipping a latte. I was avoiding being locatable. I was interested in the faces of strangers.

It was dark when I got back to Brooklyn, some time past seven. I went to a small gourmet grocery store near the subway and bought fresh groceries: a chicken breast, rosemary, potatoes, butter, fixings for a salad. Then I went to the local video store and dawdled in the aisles before choosing an old Steve Martin comedy.

As I headed up the stairs, I flipped through Vera's mail—bills, every single one. I was glad that they were addressed to somebody else. Their return addresses spoke of holes too deep to climb out of: Visa. Michael L. Cardullo, Attorney at Law. Department of Motor Vehicles. Internal Revenue Service. Direct Student Loans.

When I got to my landing I heard the phone ringing. I knew it wasn't for me, but I still rushed to get it, dropping groceries and video and stumbling inside and down the hall to the bedroom.

"Hello?"

"Hello to you."

She was chewing gum. Loud and hard. She was at a pay phone. There were street sounds behind her.

I scratched at my leg but couldn't feel anything.

"Um, hi," I said.

"Do you realize that the size of the average white man's prick is forty percent smaller than the average black man's?" She laughed, a long low chuckle like a ball bouncing down stairs. "Uh-oh. Did I shock you? I was reading this old book my uncle Herman gave me last year for Christmas. It's about all the different races of the world." She affected a slave drawl: "Da Chinee man and da Injun and da Nigra and da Cockasian. I'll show it to you tomorrow at lunch. It's a total fucking riot."

My eyes darted around the dark bedroom.

"Hey, I'm cooking something," I said. "Can we talk later?"

She gasped. "My God. Did you forget our plans? I was

supposed to cook for you tonight! Oh well. Did you make enough for two, or should I bring my own fixings?"

"Actually, I have company."

"What company? That jigaboo artist?"

"An old friend from school. Her name is—Lola."

"Oh. *Lola*." She said the name as if she too was acquainted with her. "Of course. Somebody your own age. Hip, happening Lola." She sighed. "That must be nice. Better than hanging out with an old lady." She let out a sort of strangled sound in her throat that was supposed to be a laugh but conveyed something more complicated.

"I think I smell the chicken burning. I gotta go."

"I think I smell the chicken burning. I gotta go."

I was silent.

"All right, all right, hon. I get the hint. Say hi to Lola, your lazy-assed friend who can't take the chicken off the heat for you. Tell her she better be nice to you or I'll beat her up." Pause. "I'm kidding! And call me if you can't sleep. 'Kay, sweets?"

My voice was a small bewildered wisp. "Okay. Bye."

As I hung up, I heard music turn on in the apartment next door. Al Greene. Crackling revolutions of soul. A man's deep voice said something, and then a woman's high laughter at the joke I hadn't quite made out.

I WENT TO BED EARLY, on a grinding stomach. I'd lost my appetite when I pulled out the chicken and saw it sitting there, marinating in its own juices. I didn't watch the movie either. Instead I turned off all the lights and got in bed, but I did not fall asleep. I twisted around in the sheets, trying to get comfortable on the lumpy bed that was not mine. Every sound in the building, on the street below, was fractious. Banging pipes. A dog barking. A television either next door or upstairs—the theme song to *Diff'rent Strokes.* An airplane passing overhead, that for a minute sounded like it was plummeting toward the earth.

I drifted off to sleep at three in the morning. The telephone woke me up, a shrill, angry sound like a drawer of silverware being overturned. I watched the white phone as I lay curled up tight and fetal. The answering machine picked up with a click, and the nasal, computerized man's voice told the caller to leave a message. But whoever it was didn't. He or she just sat on the other end, recording their own breathing, and I wondered if they, she, he, could hear me where I lay in the dark, barely breathing. Wondered if they would hear me if I were to speak aloud or cough. I didn't take a chance. I stayed still and quiet and waited until the person hung up.

19

I DECIDED TO WAIT to call Ivers Greene until after the article came out. A nod toward journalistic objectivity. And so the weekend stretched before me—empty and endless. On Saturday morning, I headed to midtown and got to the New York Public Library just as the doors opened, and settled into a spot in the Rose Reading Room. I did research on the article Rula had assigned to me. I found the reporting a welcome distraction. I recalled, as I poured over the clipping file and scribbled notes into a pad, the reason I'd gone into reporting in the first place. I loved the sensation of disappearing—the delicious sense of my body fading into thin air and only my eyes remaining, two brown laser points observing somebody else's story but never being a part of it.

The story Rula had assigned me was about a "wellness group" that had recently come under suspicion for practicing brainwashing tactics in their recruitment of members. The FBI was zeroing in on their leader, Tarik Raz—a slim, dark, mischievous man who reminded me a bit of a young Cat Stevens. Raz was a former medical student from Harvard who had turned into a guru. He had been fired midway through his residency at Mass General after he was caught doling out homeopathic remedies to his patients. He bought a mansion in Lemon Grove, a suburb of San Diego, and began his own clinic and mobilization center called the Institute for the Study of Wellness and Enlightenment, ISWE. It had since blossomed into a popular alternative-health center. The group's activities were near impossible to track, due in part to the heavy security around the mansion, and in part to their method of "floating" activism. They moved around the country in a series of vans, like a rock band on permanent tour. But instead of concerts, ISWE held theatrical sit-ins outside of hospitals and government offices, and Raz gave inflammatory speeches indicting "the medical establishment." According to the article, the FBI suspected that ISWE's premises were cultlike, complete with nubile young female devotees, stray mixed-breed dogs, and love children roaming the premises. There were also rumors of an increased militancy among Raz's supporters, of violence, sexual exploitation, and corruption in his ranks.

I spent the day reading up on Raz, taking notes in my spiral reporter's notebook. He was, according to one article, the son of an Israeli soldier and a Palestinian cobbler. His parents had fled Israel with the young Tarik and raised him in the San Fernando Valley.

In one interview, Raz spoke about homeopathic medicine. He said you had to cure "like with like." My mother believed this, too. As I was growing up, whenever I complained of feeling sick, she would put on her glasses, whip out a battered black book of remedies, and ask me elaborate questions about my symptoms. She would then bring me a brown glass bottle from her cupboard and feed me sugar pellets supposedly containing poison. *Sepia. Nux vomica. Deadly nightshade.* My mother swore it was these poisons, not the sugar, that would save me. You have to give the body small doses of the problem, she explained, to remind it what it's fighting against, and to trigger it into action.

I never could tell if it was those remedies that worked, or if I just naturally got better. Later, in college, I made my mother miserable by going to the student health center whenever I felt sick and taking antibiotics and cortisone and other evils.

You'll feel better for a while, my mother warned, *but you'll see. It's a temporary solution, and it will only make things worse.*

She would approve of Tarik Raz. Maybe she already knew about him. I wouldn't be surprised.

I took breaks every hour or so to rest my eyes and stare around at the array of New Yorkers around me. The balding Indian man pouring over a physics book. A handsome, dark-haired couple pretending to work on their computers but really passing one another love notes. A buxom blonde in a tight blue dress highlighting a medical textbook, seemingly oblivious to the desiring eyes of the men around her. I found endless complexity in the faces of strangers, and peace in the hum of laptops, the indiscernible clicking of brains at work. I thought about Ivers Greene. I wondered what he would think about my article. I thought of his face and the way he'd said "You have hairy arms" to me in the café. I didn't dwell on Greta or the disturbing timbre of our conversations the past few days. Something had shifted in the bathroom of the Ritz-Carlton—or perhaps before that, though I'd been unwilling to acknowledge the facts until now. In any case, I had decided to leave that chapter of my life behind, and the less mental space I gave her from now on the better.

Over the next few hours, I learned much about the rumors that swirled around the compound in Lemon Grove. The rebirthing sessions in the moonlight, complete with "placenta"—a concoction of whipped farm eggs rubbed all over the naked "newborn" recruit. The colon cleansings given in the basement every month by the resident nutritionist. The "tribal dinners" every Friday night when they feasted on tofu together in the dining hall and played seventies rock and did "wild dancing" until the wee hours.

When I got back to Brooklyn, my neighbor Flo was standing in the foyer watching the street from behind the glass door. She was the kind of woman who launched right into familiarities with absolute strangers—at bus stops, in store aisles.

"I'm waiting for my ride," she said when she saw me. "Corky—late as usual. And you just know when she gets here she's gonna be complaining about her hair. And how it's my fault that it ain't done right. You just wait and see."

I shook my head and scoffed as if I knew what and who she was talking about.

She was dressed similarly to the last time I'd seen her, but this time she was holding a huge gift basket covered in plastic, filled with fruit and nuts and chocolates.

I opened Vera's mailbox. Beside me, Flo shifted her feet and peered out at the night, sighing with impatience. "Motherfuckin' Corky," I heard her whisper to the glass.

I turned around and started to unlock the door leading into the building's main corridor, but she called after me, "Hey, you black?"

I turned around. I was not sure I'd heard her right.

"Excuse me?"

"You black?" she repeated, chewing her gum and eyeing me up and down. "Corky and me made a bet. She thinks you're a sister."

"Well," I said. "I am."

"Hmmph," she said. "You sure got a white way of showing it."

"Yeah, um," my words petered out. I'd heard this kind of dig many times before and it always stung me as if it were the first time.

"I'm just playin'," she said, smiling now with her mouth. Her eyes remained dull and suspicious. "Want to come to a Kwanzaa party? I'm on the planning committee."

She put the fruit basket down and reached in her bag and pulled out a lime-green flyer. "Here," she said.

I thanked her and looked at the flyer as I went upstairs. A bespectacled old black man was holding a little braided black girl up in his arms, the two of them laughing. The party was next week at the Umoja Community Center on the corner of DeKalb and Washington. Refreshments would be served. I knew I would not go, but even still, it was nice to have an invitation somewhere over the holidays.

When I reached my landing, I heard the phone ringing inside. I didn't rush to get it this time, allowing the machine to pick up as I took off my coat and put Vera's letters in the giant Macy's bag in the closet. But the person hung up as soon as the machine picked up and then called back all over again.

I went to the bedroom and stood at the door, one leg propped against the other in stork position, watching the phone, my arms hugged across my chest. The machine picked up again after the fourth ring, and this time her voice bellowed into the machine.

"Hello! Earth to Rocky. Pickuppickuppickup." She emitted a long sigh. "What have you been up to all day? Where were you? It's a Saturday, for God's aching bones. What could you be doing up there? Papier-fucking-mâché? I've been calling and calling your ass."

I crawled across the floor and sat at the far end of the bedroom, hugging my knees in the dark. As she rattled on, I noticed something odd. I could still hear sounds of a street behind her on the machine. Beeping cars and shouting and music playing. A Beastie Boys song. The repetition of the lines *I did it like this, I did it like that, I did it with a whiffle ball bat!* But there was an echo effect. It was the same exact sequence of noises I could hear coming from the street below.

"So I'm thinking, let's just spend a quiet evening at home, at your place. I got some food. From the Vietcong motherfuckers around the corner. And some wine. Chilean okay with you? They had Concha y Toro on sale. And I got a present for you, too." Laughter. "Come on, Rocky. I know you're up there. I saw you go inside. I saw you talking to that old Afro-American in the muumuu. She just drove off. You're funny, hiding in the dark like a little rat. Okay. However you want to play it. I'll see you in a heartbeat. Sit tight."

There was a clattering of plastic. Then, a minute later—no, actually, it was less, twenty seconds—my doorbell was ringing. Or not so much ringing as making a continuous crackling buzz. She was just holding her finger against the button, not taking it off to give me a chance to respond. I crawled on my hands and knees into the hallway, and squatted there, on the floor, staring up at the intercom. I wasn't breathing properly, but emitting short, jagged gasps. The buzzer finally stopped. I closed my eyes and rested my head against the wall behind me.

A second later there was a beating on my door. It was the way cops beat at doors on television. Boom boom boom. She stopped after a moment and said, in an almost normal tone of voice, "Hey, kid, wipe your ass and come to the door. I'm hungry. The grub's gonna get cold if you don't get off the pot."

I slowly, quietly as I could, stood up and tiptoed to the door. I peered into the peephole. Her head looked enormous and strange. She was wearing something—a scarf—wrapped around her mouth and nose. She had her face turned away as she stared out into the hall at something, but then her face turned toward me and zoomed forward, and I jerked back and she was beating the door again. "Rocky! What's the problem? You having the runs or something? Jesus. I came all this way. You're acting crazy. Just open up."

I raked a hand through my hair.

"Open the fuck up!" She was hollering now. "I found you the goddamn apartment. Remember?"

THE SCARF AROUND Greta's mouth and nose was a kaffiyeh. She also wore the purple ski cap and the beige trench coat from the other night. On her feet was a pair of green Wellington boots. She was laden down with bags— the Vietnamese food, the wine she had mentioned, and a shopping bag from Duane Reade with a square white box inside.

"Hey, girl!" she said, beaming at me. Before I could stop

her she had sauntered past me into the apartment. “So this is the famous pad. I’ve been wanting to see it ever since you moved in.”

I stepped back. “Listen, Greta.” But she ignored me, traipsed down the hall to the living room, and began putting down her bags, taking off her scarf, her trench coat, even her boots. As she did so, she looked around at the place she had, yes, found for me.

“Huh. So this is it. Not bad, not bad at all. For the price it’s actually quite sweet.” She sniffed the air. “It doesn’t smell that bad.”

I stood at the edge of the living room. “I’m sorry, Greta. Jeez, I didn’t know you’d be coming over. I’ve got a ton of work, stuff I really have to finish up by morning.”

She shook her head and said in a quiet, strained voice, “Well, you have to eat. Everybody’s got to eat.” She began to pull the containers of Vietnamese food out of the bags.

“I’m not hungry. I mean, I already ate.”

She paid me no mind. When the food was all laid out, she left it there and began to walk around the living room, picking up objects—a Steely Dan record, the disposable chopsticks, a teacup I’d left on the coffee table—and examining them as if they were evidence. I folded my arms across my chest and clenched my jaw so hard I knew it would ache later, when I lay in the dark.

She picked up a blue vase from the mantelpiece and tossed it from one hand to another.

I stepped forward. “Could you not do that? Jiminy told me not to mess anything up, to leave it how I found it.”

“Oh calm down,” she said. “I’m not gonna break anything." She placed it back where she got it. Then, "So aren't you going to give me a tour?"

I didn't stop her as she went down the hall. I guess I had the sense, beyond the fear and the anger—irrational, I know—that she had a right to see the place because she had found it for me. A sense that it wasn't really my place anyway. I followed her down the hallway to the bedroom, still babbling about how much work I had to do. I had an interview tomorrow, I kept pleading, an interview with a very important source who could meet only on Sundays. I had to get some research done.

I stood at the doorway and kept talking as she examined the knickknacks Vera had left hanging on the tackboard in the bedroom. The postcard. The Map of the Stars' Homes. The Estée Lauder gift certificate. She examined each of them, then fingered the bedspread, as if to test its quality, and ran a finger along the dresser as if to check for dust.

After a few minutes, she glanced at me standing at the doorway and laughed. "Relax! God. I think you took Jiminy Cricket a bit too literally. I mean, you are paying rent. You might as well make yourself at home."

With that, she opened Vera's closet. My clothes huddled at one end, as if cowering from Vera's, which still hung there: The pair of platform shoes. The battered leather jacket. And the two silver dresses, with the price tags still hanging off them.

"These yours?" Greta asked, running a hand along them.

"No," I said. "Those are Vera's."

"Weird," she said. Then she pulled out the leather jacket and held it up in front of her. She laughed. "Get a load of this. Wild. I used to have one of these, back in the day."

She started to put it on.

"Don't do that—" I said.

But it was too late. She had it on, and began to walk around the bedroom laughing and saying, "I'm a Hell's Angel, vroom, vroom!"

"Put it back," I said. "It's not yours."

Greta ignored me. She bent her knees slightly and leaned forward on an invisible motorcycle. She tilted her body from side to side, as if she were leaning into sharp turns, her eyes staring straight ahead at some distant road, as she sang loudly, off-tune, ". . . *the leader of the pack* . . ."

"Take it off, Greta." My voice had raised a notch. "You're in somebody else's home, for God's sake. Those aren't your things. Now come on. Show a little respect."

Greta stopped what she was doing and glared at me. I fought not to blink or avert my gaze.

It was Greta who looked away first. She struggled out of the jacket, then flung it to the floor. I walked over to pick it up, and as I placed it back on the hanger, I heard her say behind me, "Well, for your information, subletters always snoop. It's part of the arrangement. I mean, live a little. I'm sure this chick would do the same thing if she were staying in your apartment. Shit. That's the risk you take when you leave your life behind. Have you gone through her mail? Her desk drawers? That's half the fun."

"No, I haven't. Okay?" My voice sounded crybabyish. "I'm not like that, I'm not a—"

"Shall we eat?" Like magic, her mood had normalized and switched again to something brighter. "The food's probably getting cold."

I followed her into the living room, feeling like her dog,

and sat down at the kitchen table when she pointed. The food had coagulated on contact with air, and each dish looked like a regurgitated version of itself.

She didn't seem to notice and began to shovel the food into her mouth. I could feel her watching me, but I kept my eyes fixed on a spot on the wall above her head. Had that stain been there when I moved in? I could hear her chewing, the noises of slurping and crunching. Then the sound of her uncorking the wine and pouring us each a glass. I heard her glugging hers as if it were water. Still, even when she belched, I didn't respond.

She began talking—a stream of office banter. Something about Rula Maven popping diet pills in the third-floor ladies' room. "I'm telling you, her days are numbered. I mean, she's pulling some Karen Carpenter shit. Her legs are like itty-bitty twigs you could snap—"

She went quiet. I looked at her. Her mouth was twisted into a line of worry. "What's the matter?" she said. "Why are you being so quiet?" For a moment I was afraid she might cry. Her voice was thick with emotion when she spoke again. "You've been acting funny for a while. I mean, shit, you won't even look at me."

I looked at her now. "Listen. I know you found me this place, and of course I appreciate it, but, well, I didn't say we were going to be best friends. I didn't say you could just show up like this—"

She scoffed. "But Rocky."

I threw down my napkin. "My name isn't Rocky."

Greta affected a pleading expression and pushed her plate of half-eaten food toward me, like a reluctant offering.

We were quiet. I could hear the wind pressing against the

pane, a car horn bleating down on the street like a stuck sheep, and somewhere, nearby, in the building, a man sobbing, interrupted occasionally by another man's barked scolding.

I stood up and went to the window, hoping she would catch the hint. But she just sat there in front of the cooling dish of shrimp and noodles. "I need to go to bed, if you don't mind."

Out the window I saw the drug dealer's silver Jeep. Saw an arm hanging out the window, patting the side of the car to the beat of the thudding bass.

I could feel that Greta was not moving.

I turned to face her.

She was holding a fork and I watched as she drew a line through the brown sauce on her plate, then a line on top of it, a line below it. The letter *I*. Her eyes were all wet and puffy, and there were tear streaks, just drying, on her skin. When had she cried? I hadn't heard it happening.

She cracked a slow, crooked smile that made my teeth hurt. "I got us a present. You're gonna love it."

She reached under the table and pulled out the Duane Reade bag. She took out some kind of beauty kit; I could make out a row of photographs, each showing a close-up of a different body part. From where I stood I made out a stomach, an arm, a leg, an upper lip. REMOVE UNWANTED HAIR.

Greta pulled a lavender contraption out of the box. "See, I was thinking, we can wax each other. We can make it into a little thing we do, like playing beauty shop every few weeks. Think of all the money we'd save." She pulled out the rest of the equipment and began to fiddle with plugs and plastic bags and tubes of wax as she said, "I don't know about you, but I'm starting to look like Magilla Gorilla down there."

"Please, you have to leave. It's late."

Greta ignored me and plugged the contraption into the wall. An orange light went on. Next, she pulled muslin strips out and stacked them neatly on the table.

Then she stood up and began to unbutton her slacks.

"Greta, stop. I'm serious. Let's do it another time."

She ignored me and continued to pull down her pants. Her underwear was visible now.

I raised my voice. "You have to go home."

She stopped with her pants around her knees and glared at me. "Go home now?" She looked around the apartment. "You're kicking me out of here? At this hour?"

"I have to sleep, to work."

"After I just heated this shit up? Jesus, sometimes I wonder about you. I really fucking do."

But she did as I said. She pulled her pants back up and began to slam things around, putting away the waxing contraption and the muslin strips. When she'd finished, she said, "Walk me to the subway. It's dangerous out there, you know."

Outside, a thick fog hung over Brooklyn, making it appear like a stage set for a play. The streets were empty but for the occasional hurried pedestrian, shoes clicking and face turned down against the cold.

Greta sulked as she walked, arms folded across her chest. "I hate it."

I didn't ask what, but I didn't have to.

She began to rant. "New York. This city, with all these people multiplying like rats. I hate that. And you know what else? I hate that all the black men with brains or money are looking for white pussy to validate them, and all the white dudes treat me like I'm a goddamned vacation from their real life. I hate the niggers who are always whining about how somebody owes them something when they haven't done shit to deserve it anyway. I hate all those little white cocks at work who treat me like a crack mama because I've lived a little. I hate Rula Maven, that goddamned skeletal bitch, I'd like to force-feed her a pile of horse manure. And you know what else I hate? I hate all those nappy-haired bitches who gave me such hell growing up 'cause I had light skin and long hair and they didn't. Skanky jealous ho's. Shit. And you know what else? I hate Jews. You know why I hate Jews? Because they could have been somebody. I mean, they could have been a great race, and instead they've spent so much time around the WASPs that all that mediocrity has rubbed off on them. I mean, have you ever noticed how mediocre white boys are at whatever they set their minds to? Mediocrity personified. It's like if they put the square in the square and the circle in the circle they think they deserve a goddamned Pulitzer Prize. At least niggers are not mediocre." Greta was half shouting. "I mean, we're the most extreme motherfuckers on the planet—we're either geniuses or idiots. But at least we're not mediocre like some goddamned crackers. And who else? Oh yeah. I hate Jiminy, 'cause he's a goddamned honky liar who wishes he was black. Man, if there's anything I hate, it's white people. They're all suffering from some chronic motherfucking disease that makes them say stupid shit. Whiteyisms. Like they still think we're monkeys after all the goddamned evidence to the contrary. I hate that."

Her words edged toward meaning, toward clarity, a position, then veered away. Each sentence seemed to negate itself, and my head hurt from hearing it.

"I hate this crap neighborhood. God, I hate this neighborhood. With these repulsive ghetto bitches and their endlessly replicating babies everywhere. I hate them. And the fucking honky faggots who keep moving in—trying to 'spruce things up.' Goddamned disease factories. That's what they are. Spreading their plague everywhere. I hate them. I really do."

We were at the subway now. Greta turned to face me.

"But don't get me wrong." Her voice had gone soft. "I love you." She smiled, tilting her head down as she spoke. "I love you so much it literally makes me want to throw up. I mean, it's like I'm stuffed with it—this love. I woke up the other morning and I said, 'It's too much.' Like I just wanted to stick a toothbrush down my throat and get it out of me. But I knew it was too late for that. It's not in my stomach anymore. It's in my blood and my bones and my skin. It's with me. Forever. Just like I'm with you. Forever."

Artificial heat blew up from the steps.

"Greta," I said, choosing my next words carefully. "I think we should put this friendship on ice—"

"'Greta,'" she repeated in a singsong voice. "'I think we should put this friendship on ice—'" She let out a harsh scoff. "You don't even get it. I'm the best fucking friend you'll ever have. And when all your boys, white, black, Puerto Rican, have come and gone—and mark my words, they will disappear—and Lola has sold you downriver, which she will, mark my words, when all them motherfuckers have left you high and dry, I'll be here beside you. But you're too full of yourself to see that, you're too damn—"

I hugged my arms tightly to my chest, shivering now. "I'm sorry, Greta. It's not personal." I thought of a line somebody said to me once in college, and spoke it aloud, "It's just that I'm not into women."

Greta laughed through her tears. "Neither am I, you idiot. 'Into women.' God, don't insult me with your banalities. This isn't some dyke come-on. Yuck. Don't you understand? This is about the future. We could build our own reality. Fuck all those motherfuckers. Fuck the white boys and the white girls and the niggers and the gooks. Fuck the dykes and the shirt-lifters. We don't need them. We're a new race. A new people."

"This is insane," I said. "I'm going home."

"'This is insane,'" she repeated. "'I'm going home.'"

Then she turned and trudged down the steps into the city's dark innards.

20

GRETA STOPPED HASSLING ME after that night. It was hard to believe, but the problem simply dissipated, like a thick fog suddenly lifting, leaving no trace. I saw her around the office. I said hello and she said a curt hello back, but didn't meet my eyes, and if you didn't know any better, you might have thought we'd never known each other at all.

I'd see her in the cafeteria or in the hall, and I'd remember things she'd said to me in the brief heyday of our friendship. Words and phrases conjured up by the sight of her face. *Minister of information. Xanadu. Raceless lady, you know who I am.*

She changed over those weeks. I took notice, even if we didn't speak. Her change didn't look so much like a change as a settling. She succumbed to the bad habits she'd struggled against before. She gave up on any semblance of professionalism and wore her pair of New Balance running shoes around the office, leaving her low-heeled pumps beneath her desk. She came to work with the ghostly white chalk of Clearasil on her forehead and the crust of toothpaste in the corners of her mouth. One day when I walked past her cubicle, I saw that her desk was now bare. Gone was the freebie cup from McDonald's, the row of yellowing *Cathy* cartoons she'd tacked to her headboard. She'd tossed these all out, and the desk looked as if it was being used by a temp, not a full-time staff member. Gone, too, were her sparkly seventies makeup and the vivid Winter colors she'd been so careful to dress in all fall. Now she came barefaced to the office, her hair pulled back in a bun, donning colors that would have sent Dorothea into paroxysms of rage. Mustard yellow and off-white and fiery orange and lime green that didn't flatter her. Dorothea had not lied.

At lunch, she took to sitting at the secretaries' table—the one she'd once referred to as "the pig pen," squashed between Donna, the Italian-American matronly secretary, and Lisette, the aging black redhead who worked in Human Resources.

MY LIFE, on the other hand, was taking a turn for the better. One day in December, I found myself at the edge of the beach in Coney Island with Ivers Greene. Was it a date? I couldn't be sure. I'd called him after the article came out. He'd had little to say about what I'd written except, "It didn't sound like you." Before I could feel hurt, he'd invited me out here, to Coney Island. He'd sworn that it would be fun—"like a Mountain Dew commercial" were the words he used—and as I'd gone off to meet him I had imagined us on a roller coaster together, shrieking, me clutching to my chest the big red teddy bear he'd won me.

But we'd both forgotten it was winter. Everything was shut down, and what lay before us was as sore as a hangover: burned-out neon lights, an empty video arcade, abandoned gift shops hidden behind metal grates. The stagnant Ferris wheel was covered with frost, and the roller coaster appeared to be under construction.

We stood forlorn before the DO NOT ENTER sign. A teenager with bright red acne spots and stringy black hair sat on the curb smoking a cigarette. His jacket was open, and I could see the words "Guns N' Roses" across his T-shirt.

"Some kid died there last summer." He nodded his head in the direction of the roller coaster. "Flew off and broke his friggin' neck," he said, squinting off into the distance, as if he were watching the accident happen all over again. "That ride won't be up and running for a long, long time."

We thanked him for the explanation and started away, but he called after us. "You lookin' for kicks?"

We both turned, then nodded in unison. Yes, that was why we were here. For kicks. The kid pointed in the direction of a tent a little ways down the boardwalk. "Sideshow's open this time of year. It kind of sucks. Two-headed baby looks like goddamn Kitty Karry-All. But if you're looking for kicks, it's still open—"

We thanked him for the tip and shelled out two dollars apiece to a shriveled old man with a harelip. It was a rip-off. The old man led us over to the only two attractions that were up and running: a glass case containing the two-headed baby in formaldehyde, which did look a bit like Kitty Karry-All, and a caged hut in the back of the tent holding what the man claimed was "the biggest rat in the world." After he said it, he stuck a long metal rod into the cage and poked around in the hut. After a moment, a squat, gray, beady-eyed creature the size of a bulldog came waddling out. It had patches of gray fur missing, and red sores on its hindquarters. It stared at

Ivers for a moment as if it knew him from somewhere, then scuttled back into its house.

"Oh, Jesus," I said. "What is that thing?"

"A rat," the old man said.

"Nah," Ivers said, shaking his head, dubious. "That's no rat. That's a hedgehog or something."

The old man pursed his lips, indignant, then prodded with his stick until the creature came out again. We all stared at it in silence. It didn't look like a hedgehog, and it didn't look like a rat. It was something else—nameless and pathetic. Ivers knew it, too, and we both turned our eyes away, feeling complicit in the creature's suffering.

Afterward, with nothing else to do, we bought cups of coffee and went to sit on the beach, at the top edge of the sand, near the road, in the cleanest spot we could find, holding our cups for warmth. Evidence of fun gone wrong lay all around us: a crumpled beer can, a dried-up condom that looked like a dead sea urchin, and the top half of a Russian nesting doll, her inner bodies nowhere in sight.

Down near the water, a father and son played a game of catch. Both overweight, stout, with short arms, matching crew cuts. When the son missed the ball, the father would berate him with insults.

In the other direction a figure was dressed in bright purple overalls, a baseball cap, and heart-shaped sunglasses, though the light on the beach was dim. He was holding a metal detector walking in slow zigzags up and down the sand.

Maybe it was the purple, but I thought of Greta. I'd gone to the ladies' room the day before at work and, based on the sneakers, realized that it was she in the stall next to me. Her feet were facing the toilet, with one foot raised. I got the feeling she was putting in a tampon. I was too nervous to pee and left.

"What are you thinking about?"

I didn't know how to explain. "See, well, I used to have this friend—"

"What's his name?"

"No, not that kind of friend. It's a woman. From work. She got sort of—well, fixated on me."

"A crush?"

Was that it? A romantic infatuation? No, not quite. I would have known how to respond to that.

"I don't think so. It was something else. But she stopped. She backed off. It's just—I, well, I feel bad for her sometimes. I worry about her, I guess."

He nodded and looked out at the water so intently that I turned to look, too. I half expected to see Greta emerge from the water, but there was only the gray asphalt surf.

Ivers said, "I used to have a friend like that. A girl I met at a bar one night. This skinny little white chick. After I told her I didn't want to see her again, she invaded me like a virus. She found her way into my apartment, my life. I've never experienced anything like it. Phone calls at all hours. A five-page letter every day. I'd leave to go to work at my studio and there she'd be, across the street from my apartment, just standing in the dark. Waiting. She always wore this fake fur jacket. And she would be standing there in her dirty white fur, wearing a miniskirt and cowboy boots, like some kind of crazy hooker. I'd get this sick feeling when I'd see that flash of blond hair, and I'd keep walking, pretend I didn't see her. But she wouldn't let up. She was, well, relentless."

"And what happened?"

"In the end," he said, "it got so bad I had to get a restraining order. I had to bring in the law. I never wanted to go there. But she went too far."

He looked at me. "And you know what? It worked. The police only had to warn her once, and then she disappeared. Poof. Just like that."

He picked up a fistful of sand and let it sift through his fingers. "The crazy thing is, I miss her. Not the good kind of missing. I mean, I'm glad she's gone. She was a complete fucking nightmare. But when you have a friend like that, you're never alone. It's hard to explain."

"Well, I don't miss my friend," I said. "Not one bit."

He looked at me and smiled. "But she's not really gone now, is she?"

A shout like an answer came from far away: "Chicken shit! I'm gonna kick your fat ass when we get home."

We both looked to see the fat boy crying. The ball had been washed out to sea. His father hit him upside the head and he stumbled sideways.

Ivers sighed. Then said, "What do you think will happen to that kid?"

"He's gonna end up like that," I said, gesturing toward the other end of the beach, where the man with the metal detector sat on his hands and knees, digging. "Weebles wobble but they don't fall down."

Ivers chuckled and reached over and ruffled my hair. I liked the feel of his hand on my head, but it didn't stay there. He pulled it away. A shadow of darkness fell just then across the beach, and it began to rain, drops hitting the ocean like applause. Neither Ivers nor I moved. The garbage and the crappy boardwalk disappeared, and everything grew indistinct, like a commercial in soft focus. The boy and his father ran off, arms around each other, toward their car, as if all that cruelty had just been a performance.

I looked at Ivers.

"You're shivering," he said. "You'll get sick. Come on." He touched my cheek and his fingers were warm and oddly dry.

I stood up beside him and he buttoned up my coat, which was soggy now. We began to walk along the beach toward the street we'd come in on. When I glanced back, I saw the purple-overalls man was still there on his hands and knees, digging for loose change, oblivious to the pouring rain.

21

I SAW IVERS again a few nights later. We went walking along the East River during a snowstorm. The water was the color of gunmetal. Beside us, cars droned along the FDR Drive. Each snowflake was visible in the beams of headlights. I felt frighteningly happy. I had survived a rough beginning in the city, fallen in with the wrong people. But all that was over. Ivers was both weirdly familiar to me and at the same time a stranger. I was home and yet I was not home.

He told me a story of his life as we walked. He said he had been born in the Watts section of Los Angeles with scales all over his body, like a lizard. His mother was ashamed to show him to anybody. But when he turned two, the scales fell off and he grew into a chubby and cute little boy. For a while, everybody loved him. But then he kept growing wider, chubbier, way beyond cute.

"I was the fat kid. Morbidly obese." He said it soberly, like a confession. "I was that rotund guy with the pinhead, leaning against the corner store, laughing so that nobody would hate me for taking up so much space."

"How did you lose the weight?" I shouted into the wind, glancing at his lanky form. He walked bent over, his head bowed against the cold.

"Staples. In my stomach." He shrugged. "But I'll always feel fat inside. No matter how skinny I look to you."

"I don't believe you," I said, turning to face him.

With two fingers, he stretched the skin on his cheek. "Feel this," he said. "It's all extra. I used to fill it out, but now it's just hanging there."

I pulled the skin on his cheek. It felt normal and snapped into place when I let go. I put my hands on my hips. "Seriously," I said. "Can't you just tell me who you are, seriously?"

He grabbed my hand and stared at it, turned it over in his hands, as if he was examining a piece of fruit for sale. He pulled me closer to him after a moment and my face went warm with anticipation. I closed my eyes, parted my lips, and waited.

But in the very next instant, the air was filled with apocalyptic sounds. The screeching of brakes. Horns honked furiously. I turned to see a black limousine spinning in circles on the FDR. It was really going wild, like a dog chasing its tail. I grabbed Ivers's arm as the car pirouetted one last time, then landed face-first in a concrete divider.

Steam rose from the crumpled hood.

"Holy shit. Should we go help?"

"Not unless you want to die trying."

He was right. Cars whipped past in brutal procession between us and the accident.

The door to the driver's seat was opening.

A leg emerged first, then its owner: an obese white chauffeur wearing a tuxedo.

He wandered around his car in a slow circle, pausing at each tire to kick it. Afterward he just leaned against the car, staring out into the road. It seemed as if he was looking right at us where we stood on the other side, and I raised my hand, but he didn't wave back. He pulled a pack of cigarettes out of his pocket, lit one up, and stood there smoking, still watching us.

"Were you big like that?" I asked, though I still didn't believe him.

"Just like that."

After a few minutes, the man dropped his cigarette into the snow, climbed back into the battered limousine, and after a few failed revving attempts, miraculously started the engine up and screeched away with his hood smashed in like a broken nose.

"Want to come over?" Ivers pointed in the direction of a cluster of dreary buildings in Chinatown. "I have board games and soda pop."

HE LIVED in an old factory loft with high tin ceilings and a concrete floor. The signs of life were minimal, hard-edged, utilitarian. The few objects that did suggest a human presence were crushed into a corner as if ashamed of themselves: A twin bed with a rumpled red wool blanket. A green-and-yellow-plaid couch. A chintzy white dresser, on which sat an Afro pick, a bottle of Jergens lotion, an asthma inhaler. A small card table on top of which was a hot plate, one cup, one fork, one knife, one plate, and one bowl. One can of pork and beans, a bag of Ruffles potato chips.

Beside his bed lay a giant medical book; it was open to a photograph of shingles.

The rest of the space was dominated by his work. Canvases stood tilted against the walls, a few even spread across the floor. Hospital X rays he'd vandalized—shiny gray slides he'd marred with streaks of color and words and symbols.

Money signs. Hello Kitty. A Star of David. The lyrics to old songs. The X rays were so cluttered you could barely make out the original image—the original injury.

He'd also taped some of the X rays up to the window—in place of shades or curtains. They fit perfectly into each of his loft's square windowpanes.

"My friend Charlie works in a hospital. He pilfered them from the X-ray room. They're for my show. The one you wanted to know so much about. I'm almost finished. Just one more to go."

He looked around the room, appearing at once manic and exhausted as he took in the works that had so clearly taken over his living quarters, possibly his life. His expression teetered between pride and horror. He moved around the space, pointing at each piece, naming each one as if he were introducing me to a room full of friends.

"This one here is Spina Bifida. And this one, with the yellow lines, is Duodenal Ulcer. I just finished her last week. This is Fractured Femur. One of my early ones. And this is Lymphoma."

"They're—" I tried to think of a compliment. "Gruesome."

"Yeah?"

"Yeah, they're—grotesque. Sick."

"Thanks. That means a lot to me."

I was all of a sudden terribly hot. I suspected I smelled, too. "Could I take a shower?"

The bathroom was really just a shower stall with a toilet in it. The water sprayed directly into the toilet seat. But it did the trick. I felt my extremities come to life under the hot stream. I scrubbed myself clean with soap he had, an industrial bottle of antibacterial hospital soap.

I came out wrapped in a towel. Ivers was standing by the window. The lights were dimmer.

He'd made up a bed for me on the plaid couch. I asked him for pajamas.

He brought me a pair of pale green hospital scrubs with the words "New York Hospital" printed in faded red letters across the chest.

"Your buddy Charlie?"

"Yeah, he gives me a lot of free shit."

He went to the far end of the room, stared out the window. "Go ahead. Change. I won't look."

When I was done, he shut off the light and changed his own clothes in the dark, before slipping into his bed across the room.

"YOU WERE WHIMPERING like a dog in your sleep."

"Was I?"

I sat up. The dream was still with me. Fragments. Standing on the deck of a ship watching the shoreline grow thinner. A woman whispering a joke I didn't think was funny in my ear. A group of children singing a round. John Jacob Jingleheimer Schmidt.

Ivers was just an outline in the dark, seated there on the edge of the couch. His hand rested on my foot.

"What were you dreaming about?"

I shook my head. "I don't know." I shivered and stared around at the mad objects that filled his room.

"You want to sleep in my bed?"

Stiffly, I slept beside him. Barely touching.

I woke in the morning to see not the sunlight or the sky

or even the November rain. The loft was shrouded in a murky gray light, thanks to the X rays on the glass. The night before they'd appeared black—but now, with the light streaming in, I could see a fractured hip bone, a shattered wrist, the inside world of somebody's head, where a dark shadow hovered at the edge of the picture.

22

I SAW HER one day in January. I was standing in line at a bodega on Atlantic Avenue in Brooklyn. I glanced out the window and there she was, just beyond the glass doors. It looked like her, walked like her, dressed like her—but it seemed unlikely that it really, indeed, *was* her.

It was a Saturday, two weeks after Christmas. The whole city felt let down, disgruntled, as if nobody had received the toy they wanted. I had spent the actual day with Ivers and his friends—an antiholiday of artists and itinerants in Harlem. I couldn't help thinking, as I sat at the makeshift table holding the Chinese food and looking into the faces of the motley group Ivers called friends, that my parents would approve. We drank Campari and I found myself melting into their wilderness as if I'd never left home at all.

Now here was Greta. I slipped out of line, abandoning my basket of food. The bodega sat on the same block as a mosque, and at the moment I stepped out the door, the call to prayer filled the winter air, a shrill and haunting holy song that reminded me of my father.

She was halfway down the block now, holding a dog on a leash. She had never told me she had a dog. She paused now to let the beast do its business. She wore sweatpants and a dirty white parka I'd never seen before, and slapped an empty plastic bag against her leg while she waited. I watched as the dog scratched at the concrete as if to cover its mess; then Greta bent down to pick it up in her bag. She looked around for a trash can, but there was none, so she carried the shit for the next block, me trudging along behind her.

The dog kept trying to stop and sniff trash, and she kept yanking it, cursing it.

The rest of the way, I kept a safe ten-foot distance, slipping behind cars and telephone poles when the need arose. I followed her to a block where the white people ended and the Puerto Ricans began. Followed her to a single clapboard house with pale blue shingles on a street where nothing matched, a helter-skelter of businesses and dilapidated homes. A brownstone here, a dentist's office there, a bodega on the corner. And then this house.

I stood watching as she went through the gate, threw her cigarette stub behind her onto the sidewalk, went up the steps and into the left door.

I looked around. Nobody was paying any attention to me. Boys with pit bulls stood in an excited huddle. Old men played cards sitting on milk crates in front of the bodega. I walked up to her house and paused outside the gate. Pretended to be tying my shoe. Looked left. Looked right. Then I went through the gate.

But instead of going up to the front door, I scooted beside the building. I moved along the thin strip between houses, just below the first-floor windows.

When I got to the third window in, I heard the muted sound of television just above my head. I heard voices—but the words were garbled. All I knew was that one of them belonged to Greta. I stood on my tiptoes, but the window was too high. So I scavenged in the alley and found a milk crate, just like the ones the men in front of the bodega were sitting on. They grew these things in Brooklyn.

An old white lady with Greta's face sat in a wheelchair, barking in German at Greta, who lay on the sofa in her sweatpants, holding a bag of Cheetos and switching stations with the remote control. Her parka lay like a fallen beast on the floor nearby. She was ignoring the old woman, who, I assumed, was her mother.

The living room was drab fifties décor. A plaid wool couch decorated with tiny lace pillows.

Greta shoved Cheetos into her mouth as she changed the channels. Her expression, which was as sullen as an irate fifteen-year-old's, settled into a satisfied smile when she saw something she liked. She dropped the remote control to the floor and nestled into her pillows. The old lady in the wheelchair was not finished, though, and kept speaking at her in fast, guttural German. Greta ignored her.

The dog wandered in just then, his leash still dragging behind him, and began to nibble at the neon orange crumbs Greta had dropped on the floor.

When Greta noticed what it was doing, she stuck a leg out and kicked the beast so that it screeched in pain and walked away. This enraged the old woman further, and she began to roll around in her wheelchair, still yapping at Greta, working herself up into a frenzy. I thought she'd pop an artery. Instead, she rolled herself in front of the television screen and sat there, blocking the show, still speaking and waving her arms.

Greta lay for a while, staring at her mother with unfettered hatred. When she broke her gaze, it was to lean down and pick up the remote control, point it at her mother's face, and click a button.

The sound did go off—on her mother and on the television set behind her. The old woman stared, silently, unblinking, at Greta, her face rigid with fear or hatred, I couldn't tell which.

Just then, a phone rang in another room. The old lady started to roll herself toward the door, but Greta was too fast. She jumped to her feet and shoved the old lady's wheelchair out of her way, racing past her into the darkened hallway. She caught it on the first ring.

The dog, who had been lying in a corner since Greta had kicked him, dared to get up now, and he went to the old lady, wagging his tail. She leaned forward and let him lick her face, which I couldn't see but imagined to be tear-stained.

Only then did I step down and creep away.

When I got home, I took a long hot shower and stood under its stream with my eyes closed.

Stories drifted my way.

One afternoon, Rula had gone down to the fact-checking corral to ask Greta a question, and was leaving a Post-it note when she glimpsed a pair of sneakered feet sticking out from under the desk like those of the Wicked Witch of the West. Rula panicked, thinking Greta had fainted or collapsed or died, until she heard the snoring. She woke Greta up with a gentle kick of her stiletto heel and led her to her office and spoke to her behind her closed door. Fifteen minutes later Rula opened the door, looking pinched and flushed with embarrassment or maybe rage, and Greta lumbered out, a sheepish smile on her face.

I heard it from the reporters at my table. We were having lunch in the cafeteria, and they whispered about the incident in tones of jovial titillation.

"Her days are numbered."

"Maisie Roosevelt said she spends her days getting her nails done, or sitting at her desk reading poetry books from the library."

"Katie Mondello heard her throwing up in the bathroom. Right after lunch."

"Laurel Davies said she saw her feeding the pigeons in Washington Square Park last weekend. She was dressed like a bag lady and she was listening to a transistor radio and eating a Middle Eastern wrap that was dribbling all over her shirt."

I picked at my salad and stared across the room at her, where she sat alone, by the window, eating a piece of chicken with her hands. She wore a faint smile, and raised and lowered her eyebrows as if in polite conversation with an invisible friend.

IN EARLY FEBRUARY, Carlos the mailman left propped up on my desk a letter postmarked from Hawaii. On the back was my brother's familiar, loopy script. It was peppered with words I could not understand. *Phat barrels off of Kona . . . totally stoked . . . catching burly waves . . . the shit was rickt . . . kelp monster . . . Spyder caught da kine wave, brah! . . . nip factor high . . . macking . . . Quasimoto . . . I kicked that dude Vincent Cho's ass. You shoulda seen his faucet nose gush.*

23

VERS AND I WENT OUT to shop for records in the Village one day. We went to a little hole-in-the-wall that on one side sold comic books and on the other vinyl. There we stood for hours, flipping through old album covers—Rick James, Teena Marie, Patty and Tuck, Lisa Lisa and Cult Jam—artifacts of the eighties culture we had grown up on.

Afterward we walked down Lafayette toward the Lower East Side. He'd bought a Luther Vandross album. I'd bought the Dazz Band. It was four o'clock, and at the edge of the sky I could see it was getting dark. I kept my arm linked in Ivers's and babbled about something I'd seen on television the night before—a new sports show that pitted beast against man. I had watched as they'd shown a giraffe racing a human being. The human being had won without much effort.

Ivers interrupted me at some point with a whisper. "Check it out! WASPs!" He said it as if he were a bird-watcher and had just spotted a flock of rare egrets.

It was a band of white people, our age, their arms linked, singing Jane's Addiction together into the evening air. "*She gets mad, she starts to cry. She takes a swing but she can't hit.*" These were not just white people. They were a particular breed of WASP that was maybe dying off. They were handsome and rich and timeless—they moved as if they owned the city. I squinted. They were familiar. Sophie and Tommy and Chloe and some kid I didn't recognize. And yes, there at the end was Andrew. He looked somehow scrawnier than I'd remembered him. They moved forward laughing and singing, passing a small silver flask between them, the Rat Pack minus Sammy.

I stopped. Ivers looked back and forth between me and this pack, waiting for an explanation. They were upon us now, about to move past. I waited for each moment to play itself out: for Andrew to recognize me. For him to step forward and say a painful hello. And indeed, he did glance my way now, still singing into the frigid evening air. *Jane says, She's never been in love, no. She don't know what it is. She only knows if someone wants her!* His eyes glided across my face, over to Ivers's, and I waited, breathless, to see how he would greet me. But there was no flicker of recognition. And then they were all past us, leaving a faint smell of gin behind.

In late February she was turning in fact-checked articles, signed off, but she had not in fact done any checking—not a word.

She had fudged some important facts on her résumé, too. Rula and Ward were investigating further.

Her hair was falling out. In chunks. I glimpsed a faint balding at the back of her head when we passed one day in the hall.

She was spotted walking down the hall carrying a giant maxipad in her hand. She'd not bothered with discretion.

For breakfast, she ate Pop Rocks and Coke at her desk, the sizzling sound audible all over the Pit.

ONE DAY in early March I bought a new coat on my lunch hour. I was tired of wearing Vera's old ugly one that made me look like an armadillo. The one I bought was expensive, wool, a bright blue that reminded me of the sky back home. I stuffed Vera's old one into the shopping bag and wore the new one back to the office.

I sensed something was off before I even stepped inside the lobby. It was the way everybody was turned in one direction.

I went inside. A commotion. The sounds came from the farthest end of the lobby. Two security guards were struggling to drag her out of an elevator.

"Don't you touch me. Don't fuckin' touch me or I'll make you sorry your black ass was ever born."

Everybody—the shoeshine man, the newspaper kiosk owner, people on their way in and out of the lobby—had stopped what they were doing to stare. The guards finally managed to carry her out. They held her between them by her elbows.

"You see this shit? See how they treat me? Sic a couple of bona fide Negroes on me. Throw me out on the sidewalk without batting a motherfucking eyelash. This is what they call progress—"

She thrashed from side to side, bucked her whole body forward and back, but the guards held on tight. On her feet she wore her old filthy sneakers. Her skirt was ripped. Her hair was tangled and her pink lipstick smeared.

I hid beside a magazine rack, fixed my eyes on a tabloid cover. Liza Minnelli was a hermaphrodite. A piece of Michael Jackson's nose had fallen off during a concert. I tried to focus. But it was no good. She glimpsed me when she moved past and said my name.

I peeked up, my cheeks burning.

"Listen. Please. You gotta help me." Her voice was ragged, wheezing. "Just meet me outside, I need to talk—"

I couldn't hear the rest when the door closed behind them. My heart was still slamming around inside of me. I stared at the magazines on the rack, but no longer saw the words.

THAT NIGHT Ivers and I had sex at my place. His skin smelled of something chemical, sharp but not unpleasant. He'd been working all day on a mural on a wall on the Lower East Side. There were flecks of silver spray paint on his hands and cheek, like something stripped of its artifice. His breath smelled of coffee. I tried to concentrate on the act itself, but my eyes kept opening to peer around the bedroom behind his head. The Map to the Stars' Homes and the Estée Lauder gift certificate. The dead orchid. The postcard with the six puppy dogs peeking out of the pickup truck. I closed my eyes as he moved inside me, imagining Vera in this very bed, beneath one of her boyfriends. I wondered if she was loving anybody tonight in London. And was he loving her back?

When it was over, Ivers rolled off me and saw my face. "What is it? What's the matter? What did I do?"

I shook my head. "It's nothing. I'm just in a weird mood today, I don't know why."

"You look—I don't know, odd. Pale. Come on. Spit it out. What happened?"

I was quiet for a while, staring at the postcard of the puppy dogs on the corkboard, trying to think of an answer.

"I want to move," I finally said. "I think this apartment is making me sick. Is that possible?"

He was silent, and when I turned to face him, I saw he'd already fallen asleep.

24

HE HEADED OFF to Rotterdam in the second week of March. Two of his pieces had been selected for a show there. It was a big deal, and he knew it, and he was tense, distracted, at Kennedy Airport that Sunday. He looked handsome in his battered black jacket and red scarf. He held my hand, but his mind, I could see, was already six hours ahead, in The Hague.

We kissed good-bye, then waved at each other as he walked through the metal detectors. I watched his bobbing brown head till it was out of sight, then went and found the airport bar and sat there for a while, nursing a Bloody Mary and feeling generally sorry for myself to be left alone in the gloom of March. I imagined Ivers meeting a willowy blonde and never coming back.

I went to a movie at an art house in Park Slope. It told the story of an English family living in the countryside, who one rainy night hear a knock at the door. They open it to find a very pregnant blond waif standing in the cold. She is lost, her car has broken down, and she wants to know if she can spend the night. The couple, who have four children, agree to let her, but when they wake in the morning the woman is gone—having given birth in the night and having left behind her newly born baby. The couple decides to keep the baby and raise it as their own. But the adopted child is possessed, and over the next ten years she grows into a little blond angel who murders, one by one, her siblings. The film was terrifying the way only movies made in the seventies on a low budget in the English countryside can be. Everybody had bad teeth and there were odd stretches of silence when the trembling camera would zoom in on the lovely blond girl sitting in the meadow, smiling.

It was already dark when I stepped out of the theater, and in those few hours it had begun to snow. People rushed past, bundled up. The temperature had dropped. I looked for a gypsy cab, but there were none. I was wearing Vera's coat again. The new one—the fancy one—had turned out to be more for style than function. It was too cold to wear anything but the armadillo. I zipped it up and started down the hill.

I felt mild dread as I walked, but put it down to the lingering effects of the movie—and the knowledge that I was once again alone in the world. I didn't want to go back to the apartment. The space depressed me. Every month I sent a check to Jiminy. But I never heard anything from him, and the bills for his cousin were mountainous. With Ivers around I could avoid going there most nights. I hadn't been back all weekend. I kept a toothbrush in his loft.

I passed a storefront church and paused to glance inside. It was just a fluorescent-lit room, bare bones, the ugliest church you ever saw, but the people were beautiful. Old ladies in all white. Matronly women in plumed hats. Little boys in three-piece suits. They were all crowded in there, on folding chairs, backs to me, before a makeshift pulpit. On it, an old man ranted and raved. He had a salt-white Afro, a craggy face, and wore a brown suit and horn-rimmed glasses that made him look like a ghost from another era. I stood fogging up the glass, listening to his muted sermon float out, punctuated by Amens from the congregation. *Now Jacob loved Joseph more than all his children, and so he done gone and made Joseph a coat of many colors. (Amen.) And when his brothers saw that coat, Lord, they was jealous and hated their brother. And one night, Joseph dreamed a dream, that he was the ruler of them all, and he told it to his brothers—and my people, don't you know? They hated him all the more. They hated him for his dream and for his words and for the very fact of his being. (Tell it!)*

My father had attended a church like this as a child, deep in the bayou of Louisiana. Now he was halfway across the globe, in Mecca, searching through the sands for another god who would take him home. He had never told me about the terrible power of these services or the contemporary stories they spun from ancient texts. Both he and my mother had wanted a clean break from the past when they moved to California. They both believed in ruptures and amnesia and had tried to instill in my brother and me a sense of freedom from all tradition.

The old man's voice seemed to shake the glass. *And one day Joseph's own brothers threw Joseph into the pit, yes they did. (Lord no!) They threw him into a pit with no water and they took his multicolored coat and they dipped it in goat's blood and brought this coat to their father and told him his youngest son was dead. (Make it clear!)*

I wanted to hear the end of the story and dawdled outside the church for a few more minutes, but the weather was getting worse all around me. I took one last look, then continued on my way.

I FOUND FLO loitering by the mailboxes again. She was flipping through bills, and smiled up at me through her huge bifocal glasses. A huddle of plastic grocery bags brimming with food sat on the floor around her feet, along with a puddle of water from the melted snow.

She was blocking Vera's mailbox. I waited, shivering and wet, hoping she'd get the hint and move. I hadn't been home in days, and I knew it would be crammed with the usual demands for payment.

Flo stood where she was and started talking about people I didn't know. "I was supposed to go to New Jersey tonight, to go see Harold and Neecie? But it's just too wild out there." She nodded toward the outside world, the icy bluster. "It's supposed to go on all night. Maybe longer. But I've bought enough food for a week. And candles. Just to be on the safe side. You never know."

She squatted beside me and began to shove her mail into one of her grocery bags.

I stepped over her, but when I unlocked Vera's box, I found it empty. I felt a small foolish relief, as if it were I who was out of debt.

Behind me, I heard Flo's voice. "So I see your girl came home."

"What?"

"Vera," she said. "She's back."

Vera. Back. I was glad Flo couldn't see my face.

She carried on behind me, a casual banter. "I saw her in the hall a few hours ago, putting out some trash. Guess it didn't work out so well overseas." She chuckled. "From the looks of things, none of that European *sophistication* rubbed off on her. She looks like the same old greasy ho bag to me."

I shut my eyes. Swallowed. So Vera had come home the way I had always suspected she would—one night, without warning, the failure of her experiment in international living behind her. For some reason—pride, I guess—I didn't want Flo to know that this was a shock to me. I didn't want her to know I was homeless.

I gathered my wits and let out a small laugh as I turned to her. "Yeah, can you believe that? She came home early. I've gotta start looking for a new place to live."

Flo stood up and massaged her lower back. "Say, hon? Can you give me a hand with these grocery bags? My sciatica's acting up. 'Preciate it." She didn't wait for my answer and handed me the two heavier bags.

It was just as well. I needed a few minutes before I went back to the apartment for the inevitably awkward encounter. An excruciating thought crossed my mind: Had Jiminy even told Vera she had a tenant living there?

As we went up the stairs together, Flo chattered, throwing glances at me over her shoulder. "I wish you didn't have to move out. You just seem like the nicest girl. Wish we could all find a way to get rid of that Vera. Maybe I'll start a petition or something. Yeah, maybe me and Corky and Mr. Douglass—'cause he been complaining about Vera for years. Maybe we'll start us a petition and get her ass evicted."

I didn't comment. I knew they would do no such thing. It was just talk. And besides, the apartment did belong to Vera. I had no claim to it. The fact of the matter was I had nowhere to live. Vera would probably let me stay for tonight, but that would be it. And anyway, I wouldn't want to stay longer. The apartment wasn't big enough for a roommate.

Flo's apartment was on the fifth floor, just below Vera's. When we reached her landing, she set down the bags and started looking through her purse. "Now, just hold up a minute. I'm going to need your help bringing these in. My sciatica—" I could hear cats mewling from behind her door.

After an inordinate amount of time, Flo finally managed to open the door.

Two cats meandered out of the apartment and whined at the sight of Flo. She baby-talked to them—Pickles and Luigi were their names—while she picked up her few light grocery bags and started inside the apartment. I followed her with the heavy ones.

The decor was a mismatch of warring styles, but the prevailing two themes were Afrocentric and 1970s arts and crafts. African warrior masks warred with flowery bric-a-brac. A row of porcelain dolls in hoop skirts were lined up on the mantelpiece, beside a Yoruban fertility symbol. On the wall, beside a bright red, gold, and green Kwanzaa poster, hung a huge patchwork quilt. The words "Friendship Lasts Forever" were embroidered on one of the squares.

Along the wall there were traces of Flo's earlier life—photographs of a much younger Flo with rather sweet features and her hair in a short natural, seated in a group of long-haired white women. In one, the women sat before a WOMEN'S HEALTH COLLECTIVE banner.

The cats multiplied before my eyes. I counted fifteen in the living room alone. They were draped over the sofa and the kitchen table and the television set. The place smelled strongly of cat shit.

As we moved deeper inside, I saw the layout was the same as Vera's. But while Vera had furnished her place minimally, Flo's was stuffed with extra furniture—two of everything, it seemed—along with boxes and garbage bags of junk that lined the hallway so that I had to edge through as if in a tunnel. There were two huge sofas, one black leather and modern, the other pale and overstuffed, upholstered with pastel flowers. They faced one another, and between them sat two coffee tables, one glass, the other solid oak. By the window, two kitchen tables were pressed together, surrounded by a bevy of unmatched chairs.

Flo was busy feeding the cats on the kitchen counter. They prowled around the groceries, sticking their noses in the bags. Flo fed them anchovies by hand, one by one, from an open tin. Oil dripped from her fingers.

"Why do you have two of everything?" I wondered aloud, my eyes taking inventory of the room. I was loitering, I knew. Avoiding my situation. "Two couches, two tables, two television sets, two stereos . . ." My voice trailed off.

Flo glanced up from her task. "Oh, I had a roommate once. Maxine Feldman. She got all spiritual on my ass and moved to Tibet and left all her stuff behind. I decided to just keep it."

I jumped as something touched my ankle. More cats had prowled out of the bedroom and they rubbed up against my pant leg.

Flo purred to the cats on the counter before her. "Marvin, Sula, Assata, Amiri, did you eat your Tender Vittles? Come here, you big fat fish-eyed fools."

I set the grocery bags on the kitchen table. "Well, take care," I said grimly. *Because tomorrow I will be gone,* was what I thought.

One cat climbed up Flo's dreadlocks, as if they were the branches of a tree, while another stood on the counter eating tuna fish right out of a can. "Won't you stay for dinner, though? I was going to make greens and some black beans and rice, healthy stuff."

Disgusting as those cats were, I was almost tempted to eat with her. But upstairs, I heard dull footsteps. I would have to face it sooner or later. "No, thank you," I said. "I've got to go deal with Vera."

"I don't envy you," Flo said. "She's a mess, that girl. They done tried to evict her three times, for skipping out on the rent, but every time she ends up finding the money at the last minute. And the noise. Jesus! The last months have been a vacation for the building. You were so quiet! Like a little mouse. That's what Corky called you. 'The little mouse.'"

"Thanks."

She was chopping up anchovies now. I couldn't tell if they were for her dinner or for the cats. The creatures prowled in circles around her legs, purring, their tails rigid with excitement as the fishy smell wafted through the air.

"Anyway," she said, "I complained to Mr. Hinton, the super, a few times last year, about Vera and her ruckus. But he wouldn't listen. That old dirty dog is probably fuckin' the bitch. Probably got some kind of arrangement. That's how these skanky white girls stay in business, you know."

She continued muttering to herself even after I had said good-bye and started down the hall. The last words I caught as I went out the door: "And that trailer-trash music she be playin' till all hours of the night? Lordy be, I'm gonna have to invest in some earplugs."

25

I PAUSED IN THE HALLWAY, listening to her voice seep out to me from the living room. She was singing along to soul music, this girl whose home I had temporarily called my own. She had a smoker's voice, husky, androgynous, a bit ragged, like I had imagined it would be. Beneath the Curtis Mayfield, I could hear a faint tearing sound, like newspaper being slowly shredded.

My old coat—her old coat—was soaked through, and I saw I'd created a puddle of wetness on her hardwood floor. I felt a wave of shame at the sight—as if I were a lost puppy who had wandered in off the streets to urinate indoors. The song came to an end and there was nothing except the tearing sound.

I knocked my fist against the wall beside me, just to get her attention. But there was no reply. I called out, "Hello! Is somebody there?" But still no reply—just the intermittent sound of tearing. I crossed my arms, shrugged to nobody, and started down the hall to meet her.

SHE WAS WEARING one of my old oxford shirts from the closet and a pair of running shorts that she must have found in my suitcase.

She sat beneath the *Mahogany* poster, her legs stretched out before her.

The wax strips she had already pulled off lay faceup all around her. They looked like grass beds, holding the prickly black hairs she had just torn from her body.

A pile of fresh muslin strips were stacked neatly beside her. Her job was only half done. One leg sat finished, a newborn babe, glowing and hairless. The other leg, which she had just started now, was still coated in straight black hair.

For a while I couldn't say anything. I just watched while she spread the wax on her leg with a spatula in the direction of the hair growth, then pressed the muslin strip against it and tore in the opposite direction, just like the ladies in the salons. She did it with expert swiftness, as if she had been trained in this art.

After a moment, she did glance up at me, without much interest, but then concentrated on the task in front of her.

"I don't understand," I said. "I thought—"

"Figure it out. You're the genius here." She continued waxing. She had finished only a few strips on the second leg, and the contrast between what had been waxed and what remained in its natural state was dramatic. It looked like a lawn half mowed, each side revealing what the other was not.

I tried to sound calm, but I heard the tremor under my voice. "So you had a key?"

"Of course I had a key," she said. "This is my place."

"What about Vera?"

"What about Vera?" She chuckled for a minute, enjoying, I guess, my surprise. "I was gonna wait a few weeks to come home—but I couldn't take another minute of that old gimp. Always on my back."

There was a fetid smell in the air, like a dying apple. I felt saliva gathering in my mouth. All around me was her mess. My eyes roamed the space. Chinese food containers sat cluttered on the kitchen table. She'd pulled some of my clothes out of the bedroom, and they lay in a tangled heap in the middle of the living room floor.

"Wait, I'm lost," I said, with a short strangled laugh. "How can that be?"

"How can what be?"

"How can you be—"

"Vera? Don't be stupid. There are a million motherfuckers out there with more than one name. Herman Schmidt a.k.a. Niggah with Attitude a.k.a. Jiminy Wendell Harris." She sighed. "It's easy. You just gotta have the cojones."

"But—" Only one word came to mind. "Why?"

She sighed. "Because I was just sick of being Vera, okay? Tired of credit card assholes calling my ass day and night. Tired of Mr. Hinton threatening to evict me if I didn't put out. You're young. You don't know this yet. But a name can get pretty fuckin' worn out in this town. It starts to lose its snap and sheen. People start thinking you owe them something just 'cause your name is Vera Cross." She ripped off a new sheet of wax and winced in pain. "Anyway, I needed money. A job. A good job. The temp agencies all had me on some list of people not to hire. So I got a new name and a new résumé. Faked some references. Faked some IDs, and voilà, I was Greta Hicks. It was no big deal. I'd done it before. But this time was different because—" She looked up at me quite suddenly. It was a look so hard and direct I coughed, just to feel something.

"Because I met you. Two of us! Two of us in that one stinking plantation. What are the odds? It changed everything. I wanted you to have what I had and to know what I knew. I would have given you everything. The coat off my back. I would have shown you the way. It wasn't a coincidence we met. You do realize that, don't you?"

When I didn't answer, she looked back down at her leg and scratched at a piece of wax that had not come off properly. "Anyway, I hope you appreciated the place. I've been staying with my mother the past few months. That old bitch was on my case every minute." Greta chuckled. "She even called the Elder Abuse Hotline one night. I didn't even know they had such a thing. Elder abuse. Jeez Louise, after all the dog walking I did for her, too. The nerve."

I was aware of being hot. Sweat drenched my underarms. It mixed with the cold wetness from the storm outdoors, making me slightly dizzy.

She eyed me from my head to my shoes. "So where were you anyway? Fucking King Kong?"

"Actually," I said, "I'm just here to collect my things. Then I'm leaving. This place. You can have it back. Tonight."

Of course, it seemed like a crazy thing to say when I looked up at the window, at the snow swirling around out there. It was the same impulse I'd had once in college, when I'd found an impossibly huge insect—a water bug—in my dorm room bed. I'd wanted to evacuate the premises rather than do the sensible thing, which was to kill the creature.

She didn't respond. She just continued waxing, spreading a fresh layer of the yellow goo along her thigh.

"Well, I'm going to pack," I said, and started down the hall. The sound of wax and hair being ripped away from skin followed me.

I stopped at the door to the bedroom. It was a disaster. In

a short time, she had been able to destroy it. My clothes and her own clothes were strewn together on the floor. The bed had been stripped, and the duvet and pillows were on the floor, in a corner, as if she'd chosen to sleep there, under the window. The Map of the Stars' Homes lay in the middle of the floor, ripped, beside an overturned cup of coffee. The brown liquid had dried on the rug. The lamp beside the bed had a tear in its paper like an open wound, and she'd ripped some of the pages out of *The Dance of Anger,* the overdue library book, and pasted them up on the wall over the bed.

And when I glanced up at the tackboard, I saw that all of her pictures and postcards had been removed. In their place, she had hung up the photo of my family. She must have scavenged through my box of personal belongings. My eyes stung when I saw what she'd done to it. She had put white pushpins in all of our eyes so that we looked like a family of zombies. There was something written on it, too, in black Magic Marker, and when I crossed the room, stepping over the mess, I saw it said "Who killed the Congo?"

I heard her voice behind me—high and breathless—an imitation of a Southern belle. "Why ah would have tidied up if I knew you were comin' ovah, Mr. Butlah."

I turned around to see her standing at the doorway, hands on hips. She wore a dirty old bathrobe, but it hung open, so I could see both her legs. They were clean now, hairless from top to bottom, and shining with some kind of oil, so they looked like prosthetic limbs.

"What have you done?" I asked, noticing new vandalism on the opposite wall. Over the dresser, she'd written in giant Magic Marker letters "XANADU."

I sank down on the radiator behind me. It was hot. But I

stayed there, letting it burn through my pants legs. I touched my forehead. "Why would you do this? I mean, if it was somebody to pay the rent, that's one thing. But this?" I swallowed. "You're sick."

She shook her head. "Don't say that. I'm not sick. I'm not. Don't you know? Without you I'm nothing—" Her voice caught, and she covered her face with her hands and began to cry. She stood there at the doorway, weeping behind her hands. I watched her shoulders shake silently, listened to the gasping noises she made behind her hands, and I felt a small awakening of pity.

"This is nuts," I said, rising from the radiator and taking a step forward. "You've got to get help. There are people who can help you. That's their job. But you've got to ask for it."

She pulled her hands away and I saw that she was not crying at all. She was laughing. Her cheeks were wet, but from tears of hilarity, not sorrow. She wiped at her face with the back of her hand and shook her head silently, drooling a little now as she quaked.

I backed up. My fingers twitched so that I had to move them. I scratched my thighs. "What are you laughing at?"

"You. You look funny. Like a monkey in a cage." She chuckled harder. "Spooked."

I reached behind me for the phone, and grasped it without looking.

"Put down the phone."

"I just need to call somebody." I began punching in random digits. I could not remember anyone's number. "My parents. They're expecting—"

"Put down the fucking phone!"

It fell to the floor with a clatter. She was moving toward me. I saw her face as ragged, much older, suddenly, than forty-three.

"Don't do this. Please, Greta."

"That's not my name. At least get it right."

"I want to go home."

" 'I want to go home. I want my mommy.' That honkified whore doesn't give a rat's ass where you are. And neither does that fat edumacated Negro daddy of yours, playing in the sandbox with a bunch of towel heads. You think he cares if you live or die? Wipe your fuckin' eyes. I'm just telling you the truth. And so what. My mama didn't give a shit about me either. My father was the only one who ever loved me and he ate bullets for breakfast. So don't even think about trying to leave. Hear me? God, stop crying and answer me. Do you hear me?"

26

SCREAMED as she lunged toward me—not a word, just a wail, warbled and plaintive. Her fist struck me across the face. My neck snapped back. Before I could recover, she had struck me again, this time in the stomach. I bent over, clutching my abdomen. I heard my own small voice say, "Please, please, no." Then a sob—was it hers or mine?—broken by a fit of coughing. I heard these sounds distantly, as if there were two of me now, one made of skin and bones, bruisable and breakable, the other just a vapor, floating above, watching the scene but unable to help. I watched as Greta dragged me by the wrist and hair into the living room. Watched as she twisted my arms behind my back and tied them with a belt she'd brought with her. Watched as she shoved me down on the sofa and stuffed a red cardigan that lay there into my mouth. Only the sleeve fit. The rest of it hung out down my front. It tasted of wool and perfume. The cloth tickled the back of my throat and my throat convulsed, but I couldn't spit it out.

"It's just you never listen," she said, breathing hard from the exertion. "Now maybe you'll listen."

She fiddled with some buttons at the stereo. The room filled with blaring rock, Steely Dan. "Hey Nineteen."

"I love this song," she said, nodding and snapping her fingers to the music. She glanced over at me. "Don't you? Don't you love this song?" She shrugged when I didn't answer. "Whatever. You were probably in diapers when this shit came out. I bet you and your man like to listen to that rap shit together."

Ivers. She was talking about Ivers Greene. It seemed centuries before that I'd waved to him from the airport security checkpoint. The thought of him brought a sob to my throat, but the sweater made it useless. It had nowhere to go.

In front of me she was affecting a dumb expression, bending her knees and bouncing up and down. "Uh, uh, nigga this, bitch that. Ho. Yo mama. Uh uh uh." She shook her head. "I hate that shit. Calling itself music."

She wandered over to the window and peered out at something on the street, then after a moment turned around to face me. She leaned against the window and crossed her arms. Observed me from across the room. "I know you're gonna blow this all out of proportion. You'll somehow make it look like my fault. That would be just typical of you. To flip it on me."

She started to walk in my direction, and I braced myself, but then the door buzzer rang. I shut my eyes, and some mixture of hope and terror pulsed through me. Help had come. Ivers's plane had been canceled because of the snow. He'd come to spend the night. But Greta just sighed as if she was expecting a visitor.

"About fucking time," she said, as she started out of the room. "And he best not be empty-handed."

JIMINY'S VOICE WAS still familiar to me, though we'd met only that one time.

"Wassup, V?" I heard him say, high and jive, down the hall. "Amadeus, this be my cuz, Vera."

A slapping of hands. A deep voice I didn't recognize. "'Sup."

They whispered together in the hall. I caught the words "out of hand" and "party hardy" and "stupid bitch thought she was going somewhere."

I tilted my body to the side so that I could peer down the hall. I wanted to glimpse this Amadeus—the one stranger present. I wanted him to see me, bound and vomiting this blood-colored garment. He would see me and he would respond. He would call the police and tell them what was going on up here.

Jiminy was dressed in the same attire I'd seen him in the last time: a huge parka and oversized pants and unlaced sneakers. Amadeus stood beside him, a scrawny white kid with cornrows. Blond cornrows, like Bo Derek's. He peered down the hall at me and seemed to meet my gaze—but didn't respond to what he saw. He only nodded to Steely Dan and looked away, back at her.

She had her hand on her hip. "So where's the booze?"

Jiminy shrugged, his palms up, and mumbled something I couldn't make out.

She shook her head. "I told your ass to bring the booze. How're we gonna have a party, you idiot, without some liquor?"

He stepped back, hands still held out. "I tole you. It's Sunday. Motherfucking liquor store ain't open—"

She cut him off. "And with all the clowns and junkies and hookers you know," she was hollering now, "not one of them could spare a fucking bottle of scotch?"

"Don't push me, V. You're pushing me."

The music on the stereo had switched to America. *Well, I keep on thinkin' 'bout you, sister golden hair surprise . . .*

"Shut your mouth."

Jiminy stuck his chest out like a rooster. "No, why don't you shut your mouth?"

She wagged her hand up in his face. " 'Cause your ass is a liar. That's why. I don't even know why you came here tonight. You think I wanted to see you so badly? You think it was your illustrious company I was after?"

I listened to their voices and stared at the darkened television. I had sat on this very couch these past months, eating my egg foo yong and gulping my Chilean chardonnay, watching one sitcom after another. Now I could see my reflection, tiny and strange in the gray-green glass. I looked pathetic with the sweater spilling out of my mouth.

Down the hall, Jiminy was sucking his teeth. "Don't talk all proper with me."

"Sorry, I forgot you're dyslexic."

"No, you did not just say that. A'ight. A'ight. Thass it. I've had it with you and your crazy-assed schemes. Every year it's a new name, a new game. But you never get far, V, do you? You always end up back here, stewin' in your own shit."

There was a sudden commotion. Somebody slapped somebody; I heard a squeaking of sneakered feet, grunting, shouts. I closed my eyes and waited for the neighbors to open their doors, to intervene. But the commotion died down as quickly as it started.

"Yo, Cricket, man, let's split," Amadeus was saying. "This party's dead as a motherfucking president. Dwayne said they hired a stripper up on Pacific Street. They got mad weed, too."

The magic words.

"No joke?" Jiminy said. "Cool. We out." As they shuffled out the door, he yelled back over his shoulder, "And don't ask me for no more favors—beeyatch."

"You're a real piece of shit, Jiminy!" she screamed out at him in the hall, before slamming the door shut.

Claude told me something else about myself. It was four months into our relationship. We were in his graduate housing suite, hanging out with his roommate, a computer engineer named Jarvis, with dark skin and a soft, Southern drawl. The living room was unlit except for a single candle burning on the coffee table. Bob Marley's "No Woman, No Cry" played on the stereo. Jarvis and Claude and I passed a joint among us until we were burning our fingertips. We were quiet, each in our own private bubble, bobbing our heads to the music, when all of a sudden Claude blurted out, "See, Jarvis, the thing about mules"—he looked at me, smirking through the candlelight—"is they can go either way. They either get the best of both worlds—the strength of the donkey and the showmanship of the Thoroughbred horse—or the worst of their lineage—the braying stubbornness of a donkey and the genetic weakness, rubbery limbs, and low IQ of an overbred horse. You just never know. It's the luck of the draw." He leaned forward and picked up a lock of my hair, rubbed it between his fingers as if he were shopping for quality bed linen, before letting it drop. "In other words, chicks like this? They either end up genius messiahs, or craven hybrid monstrosities. But they'll never be ordinary. No, sir. Bubbling away in this one's blood are the ingredients for something quite extraordinary."

"Man," Jarvis said. "Why are you talking so much shit?"

"I'm telling you. It's true!"

Jarvis looked at me. "This asshole's just messing with you. He knows full well they don't make mules like that anymore. Shit, that breed went out of style with the hula hoop. Mulattos these days are all ordinary and well adjusted. Even a little boring." He sighed, and began to roll a new joint. "Almost makes you miss the old head cases."

I HEARD her footsteps pattering down the hall toward me. They were light, like a ghost's or a child's. A moment later, she stood in the doorway, head tilted back, watching me. "I feel like I've known you forever."

She sat beside me on the couch, so close I could smell the gardenia and sweat on her skin. Her bathrobe had flapped open slightly, so that I could see her thigh where the flecks of wax had dried on her skin. She slid her hands under her thighs and rocked back and forth for a moment, biting her lip and glancing at me as if she was trying to decide whether to tell me something. Finally, she began to speak, her eyes on the coffee table.

"When I was a kid I used to lie in bed imagining that somewhere out there was a girl just like me. I could see her, lying in a bed on the other side of the country, crying into a pillow because she was all alone. And whenever I felt like a freak—the fucking half-caste misfit that everybody wanted but nobody loved—I would think about this little girl so far away and I would feel better. I used to pray for you at night, Rocky. I used to pray that you would make it, survive, you know? So that we could meet some day. Because I knew that if we could just come together, everything would be okay." Her eyes were those of an alert and feverish confessor. "You know as well as I do: It's a good game, this thing we do. I can become whoever the fuck people want me to be. I can switch from ghettoese to the Queen's English at the drop of a dime. I can shake my ass and I can do the fucking fox trot. I can make a white man feel like he's with the most bodacious black girl alive, all earthy brown sugar and grits, and I can make a brother feel like he's got the whitest white girl beneath him. I know how to please them all, but it gets tiring. You know that as well as I do. It gets tiring and, after a while, you're moving so fast, just to survive this game, you forget who you really are. The original you? That's what I forgot. Until I met you."

She turned to face me now, and her eyes fixed on a spot beside my face. Whatever she saw there seemed to me now both a total figment of her imagination and at the same time real. I could almost feel its heat and hear its breathing.

"I remember the first time we really spoke. Do you remember that? I was like, whew! We're here! It's finally happened! I met her. You. Us. God, it was crazy, wasn't it? I mean, it was like everybody else faded away. Nobody else mattered in that stupid room except you and me and that we were there, finally, together."

I tried to remember the meeting, and it seemed that she

was right, because I could not remember anybody else from that day, any other faces in that room but hers, smiling at me, eyes bright and eager, a bag of Hershey's Kisses in her hand.

"You know why you're here, right?"

I shook my head.

"Yes, you do. You know why you came back here tonight." Her eyes were shining, wet, but she was smiling, too. They didn't go together, those two parts of her face. "We're going to do it, Rocky. Tonight. We're going away. We're going to go so far away nobody will ever find us. It'll be beautiful. I promise. And we'll be together. So don't be scared. Don't be scared. Oh there now, don't cry." She wiped my tears away with her fingers. "There's nothing to be scared of. Nothing at all. I'll be right by your side. I won't let go."

SHE LED ME down the hall to the bedroom, a carving knife she'd fetched from the kitchen held up against my back.

There, she made me sit, still bound and gagged, in the corner beside the bed, while she pulled out the two silver dresses from the closet. She flung one on the bed and began to pull the other over her head as she talked.

"We're gonna have a poetry reading," she said, as she fiddled with the wraparound sash. "A poetry slam. Up on the roof, just you and me, staring down over this good-for-nothing city. I'm gonna read to you, you're gonna listen. Finally. You'll shut your trap and listen. You think I was always like this. But you're wrong. You don't know the half of it. I used to be young. I used to be just like you, cocksure and filled with so much fucking potential I nearly exploded. I'll show you who I was at your age."

She was in her dress now. It fit her awkwardly, stretching too tight across her breasts, too loose across her middle. She waved the knife at me. "Stand up."

I clambered to my feet.

She unbound my hands, pulled the gag out of my mouth. I didn't fight or scream but kept my eyes fixed on the knife.

"Put that on."

I put it on, the other silver dress. It was too small. I squeezed in my gut and zipped it up the side.

She sat on the bed. "Turn around. Do a little dance."

She held the knife lightly on her lap.

I turned in circles, slowly, dizzy, aching, tilting my head from side to side.

"Cute, real cute."

I kept spinning slowly.

"You can stop turning now."

I did. She came toward me and moved her hands around her face. "Can you do something with your hair?"

I made a show of teasing it with my fingers.

She shook her head. "Never mind, it's not doing any good. I've got to do something with your face. Jesus. I don't want this mug staring at me while I read my work."

IT WAS ALREADY FOUR in the morning by the time we made it to the roof. She held the knife lightly against my back. She'd smeared makeup on me downstairs, in the bright lights of the bathroom—sparkly blue eye shadow, hot-pink blush, magenta lipstick. My hair lay in Shirley Temple ringlets around my face. The ends smelled burned from the curling iron.

We went through the heavy metal door. Outside. It had

stopped snowing. The sky was a plum swirl against electric blue. The air was frigid, burning really, the way cold things can sometimes be. She gestured with the knife to a spot on the snow and I squatted there and tried to stop my teeth from chattering as I waited for her to begin the poetry reading.

She seemed unaffected by the temperature as she paced before me in high heels, holding a battered black journal she'd fetched from the back of the closet. She read in a breathless rush, so that it was hard to tell where one poem ended and one began.

"Broken, breaking, broke, and I'm outta dope. My cranial cavity is festering with worms, and I see monkeys in the most unlikely of places. . . . Her breath smells of peach schnapps, stomach acid, a night she can no longer remember. The Honorable Willie Coker. A man who is not a man but an object of her desire, he is being watched and he doesn't even know it. Look. Right there. Coming out of the building. Doesn't he look funny. In that judge's gown? Lien, the bills lean on me. I got a letter today, says they will garnish my wages with parsley. Chameleon, have you ever wondered how a girl disappears? You know, walks away from the bills and the bullshit. Straight up vanishes? Well lean in, sister, And listen closely, Cause I know the trick. You just take a deep breath. And jump . . . Go figure, My washcloth smells like somebody else's face and my feet are cracked with some kind of fungus. There's a fly that won't die who lives in my sink and a Mexican cockroach who sings me to sleep at night. La Cucaracha, La Cucaracha, my belly button is full of lint and there are stains like spilled tea in the crotch of my underwear. I found a single hair, thick and wiry, growing out of my chin yesterday, and some dimples that shouldn't be there on my butt. Hand me that bottle, Jiminy. I need a fix . . . Psst. Come close. I'll let you in on a secret. My best girlfriend is tiny, fits in the palm of my hand. She laughs at my jokes and cries for my pain, she lives for me only and doesn't complain. . . ."

I was aware as I listened of a million potential saviors all around us, of how the gravel sparkled with diamonds, and of how close she kept swinging to the edge of the roof as she raved on. The air smelled of kitty litter and ammonia. I could hear chanting from a house party still in full throttle. *The roof, the roof, the roof is on fire! We don't need no water, let the motherfucker burn. Burn motherfucker. Burn.* The poems kept coming. I heard a window open and a man's enraged sleepy voice shouting, "Shut the fuck up!"

At some point I looked up and saw that the sky was peach. When had that happened? Behind her, in the distance, I saw people out on Fulton Street, walking dogs, waiting for buses. And Flo. There she was, holding a cup of coffee and leaning against a car, talking to somebody in the driver's seat.

I looked back at Greta. She was pacing back and forth in a wobbly goose step, barking the poems up at the whitening sky. Her skin shone like pale wax. I began to crawl toward the corner of the roof, at an acute angle from where she stood. I would gesture to Flo. She would see me and she would understand what was happening. I would not need to say a word. I crawled, not breathing, the gravel beneath the snow embedding itself into my palms and knees. Flo was looking up just now, and I waved my arm at her. But she just sipped her coffee and looked away as if she had not seen me. Behind me the poetry had stopped. There was only silence, and then the sound of snow crunching under footsteps. I turned my face in time to see her rushing at me, knife raised. Flashes of silver. The dress. The metal. I tried to move past her, but there was a slash of contact and I felt a warm rush of pain in my abdomen. The inside. That mystery space. What my mother calls the invisible world. Then, before I could stagger off, she had me in an embrace so tight my arms were pinned to my sides. We were intertwined. My blood was seeping out into the space between us. Onto my dress, onto her dress. The blood felt warm, like somewhere I'd like to be. She was warm, too, a perfumey heat that engulfed me. We staggered around in circles this way, a crazy dance. She sobbed and tried to pull us toward the edge. That beautiful place. I tried to pull back, aware of the wetness in my middle, aware that my vision was blurring slightly. *Guess it's true what they say.* Who said that? Voices and sounds came to me from every direction. A dog began to bark. A car alarm went off. A man in a window down below said, *"Arriba!"* and laughed at his own joke.

I twisted and arched my back until finally I was able to lift my arms and push back and away. I heard her cry, first loud, then fainter, as the distance between us grew.

LATER, down on Fulton Street, after the ambulance and police cars had come and gone, after the witnesses to the fall had given their statements, after I had been questioned and believed, I stood at the edge of the crowd, my hastily packed Samsonite beside me. The wound was superficial. I'd left the stained silver dress in the basement trash, all balled up in a plastic bag. Around me, it seemed that everyone in the neighborhood had come out of their houses, settlers and natives alike. In the half-light of early morning, they sipped their coffee and chattered to one another about the tragedy, their faces ablaze with excitement.

"Hate to say it," Flo was saying to a cluster of rapt faces. "But I saw it coming. We all saw it coming. There was only one way that story was gonna end."

Beside her, Corky nodded. "Ain't it the truth?"

27

MY FATHER TELLS ME that the further you get away from an experience, the deeper it roots itself inside of you. Don't fool yourself, baby, he said. Time does not heal and history is not progressive.

My mother has other opinions. She says the soul is forged through suffering; every hardship is a lesson in disguise.

It has been five years since I left New York—five years since I walked away from that apartment, from that crowd of strangers on the sidewalk. I have returned to the city where I got lost so many years ago. I have given up on nonfiction. I am working toward the most useless of degrees. I study the art of lying. My teacher, a tall, somber woman who wrote a novel about a midget, tells me that I am "learning to inhabit the space between truth and fiction." She says that I am at my best when I lose control. "You must keep climbing into that abyss where nothing is certain. And don't worry about what really happened. It's only the logic of the lie that matters here."

I live in my own apartment now—a two-room studio on the second floor of a stained pink stucco apartment complex not far from the beach. It's drab, but it's funny how you can love something, anything, when you know it is yours. I only see what's beautiful about the place: the way the light falls across the living room in the evenings, a gold-peach rectangle that grows thinner and thinner until it is just a sliver and then gone. And the view from my patio of the ocean, only seven blocks away. It looks like a slice of fallen sky.

I don't even mind the flaws of the place, like the rust stains in the bathtub or the worn spots on the carpet or the way you have to jiggle the toilet handle to make the water stop running. Or even the way the kitchen floor sits at a crooked angle, tilted by the earthquake that shook the area a few years ago.

I live alone but I am not lonely. I have new friends from the university. Each of them comes from somewhere else. Vietnam. Ohio. Oakland. Mexico City. And old friends, too, not so far away. Lola lives across town in Silverlake, with her girlfriend. She met Bunmi on her travels, or as she likes to say, "Had to go all the way to the motherland to find me a woman." And Ivers. He ended up on this coast, too. He lives in a shack in Venice Beach. He and I are friends now. Our breakup was gradual, soft, like a metal settling into its permanent form. We see each other every few weeks. We always say we're going to go somewhere, but we always end up just driving. Not to get anywhere, just to move. We cruise through the city, pointing out what is beautiful and what is ugly about this outpost where we have landed. A billboard of a surgically enhanced blonde. A one-armed Mexican selling oranges at the intersection. The way the store signs change languages—Korean, Russian, Spanish—from block to block. Beside him, I feel that I am everywhere and I am nowhere, and what happened before seems very far away, like another girl's life altogether.

But there are other days, when I am confused. It feels closer. I wake to the sound of the sprinkler hitting the windowpane and think it is raining ice outside, and I am back in that winter city, surrounded by her objects, her perfume, her mountain of unpaid bills. Out on the street, in the glare of the afternoon sun, I see her where she is not: in the huddle of day workers waiting for the bus down to the border, or in the cool impervious smile of a Persian housewife coming out of the dry cleaner's. Even in the face of the homeless lady at the corner of Santa Monica Boulevard, with her shopping cart filled with cans—apparently a former literature professor from the University of California, who gradually lost her mind. She stands on that corner all day, yelling to whoever will listen about her lost dog. Has anybody seen her dog?

And then there was the night a few weeks ago. I was at home, watching the six-o'clock news and sipping a Corona, and I thought I heard her voice, wheezing and ragged, right outside my door. I was so certain, I muted the television's volume, closed my eyes, and just listened, my heart beating overtime. (I really thought in that instant you had found me.) But when I got up the courage to open the door, there was, of course, nobody there.